MIDNIGHT ABDUCTION

A CHRISTIAN ROMANTIC SUSPENSE

FINNEGAN FIRST RESPONDERS

LAURA SCOTT

READSCAPE PUBLISHING, LLC

CHAPTER ONE

Grace Ramsey glanced over her shoulder as she held her son's hand and walked toward her small apartment located three blocks from the day care center. Twice now, she'd glimpsed a man wearing a dark hoodie lingering near the day care, but each time she'd been about to call the police, he'd vanished.

There was no sign of him now, but she made a mental note to call the Ravenswood police anyway. Owning and operating the Bright Stars day care center meant always being on alert for predators paying too much attention to her young charges. Even seeing the hoodie man twice was two times too many.

"Mom, I'm hungry," Caleb whined. "Can we have pizza for dinner?"

"We had pizza yesterday." She glanced down at him. The May weather was mild, so Caleb hadn't wanted to wear his coat. "We're having cheesy chicken and broccoli."

"Little trees?" Caleb brightened. He was one of the few kids she knew who actually liked broccoli. "Okay."

He was a good kid, and as always, she experienced a

little pang in her chest at how much Caleb looked like his father. She'd thought she'd gotten over her guilt over not telling Brady about his son, but at odd times the truth smacked the center of her forehead.

She'd had a very good reason for breaking things off with Brady seven years ago. The reason was just as important today. Yet, deep down, she admitted that keeping him in the dark wasn't fair. Brady deserved to know.

Reaching the apartment building, she used her key to get inside, then glanced over her shoulder one last time. Still no guy in a hoodie. It should have been reassuring, but it wasn't.

After Caleb had been fed, bathed, and tucked into bed, she returned to the kitchen to call the nonemergency line of the Ravenswood Police Department. It would make her feel better to put them on notice about hoodie guy. Her description probably wouldn't help much, but at least she'd put the officers on alert. They may send squads to patrol the area around her day care center to find him.

She stared at the Mother's Day card stuck to the fridge as she waited to be transferred to an officer on duty. Maybe she should think about talking to Brady before Father's Day next month. Each year, she experienced more guilt over keeping her secret.

The Ravenswood police officer who answered her call asked for her name and address, then promised to let the shift sergeant know to be on the lookout for a man in a hoodie. She thanked him, then hung up, satisfied she'd done her part. When her phone rang again fifteen minutes later with a local number she didn't recognize, she inwardly groaned. Her apartment was on the ground floor as she was also the building manager. Every dollar had counted in those early days when she'd left Chicago, and while she may not be as strapped for cash as she once had been, she still preferred to live a simple and frugal life. Granted, that also meant getting odd calls day or night.

"This is Ms. Ramsey," she answered, fully expecting a problem with someone's plumbing or heating. Those were her most common calls.

There was nothing but silence. A chill slipped down her spine.

"May I help you?" she asked in a sharp tone. Some of the tenants were a bit hard of hearing, but this seemed off. Lowering her phone, she looked to make sure the connection hadn't been lost.

"Do you need help?" she asked again.

There was no mistaking the sound of breathing. It freaked her out so badly she quickly disconnected from the call, then blocked the number so whoever had done this couldn't call again.

The crank call put her on edge. A teenager, most likely, but still creepy just the same. She cleaned her minuscule kitchen, then headed over to pull out the sofa sleeper. The apartment only had one bedroom, and she'd given that to Caleb.

Maybe one day we'll move into a two-bedroom apartment, she thought drowsily. The day care center was doing a little better now that the pandemic was mostly over. Many work-at-home employees had been forced to return to the office. Of course, that also added a staffing shortage, but they were doing okay. And there was one tenant in a two-bedroom apartment on the third floor that hadn't renewed her lease that would be up in August.

Sheer survival had been a part of Grace's life for so long it seemed strange to consider something so luxurious as a two-bedroom apartment. She had a month to decide whether or not to take it.

A muffled cry woke her from a sound sleep. Caleb? She rolled off the sofa sleeper. The clock on the microwave indicated it was midnight. Blinking in the darkness, she hurried to his room. Her son didn't have nightmares often, but when he did, he usually cried out her name. The muffled sound was unusual.

"Caleb, honey, it's okay." She pushed open his door. The nightlight in the corner of his room was out, and she realized that might be the source of his anxiety. She crossed to the bed, putting her hand on the mound of covers.

The bed was empty.

Alarm raised the hairs on the back of her neck. "Caleb? I'm here. There's no reason to be afraid." He might have gone into the bathroom. She flipped on the lights, wincing at the brightness before she realized the window was open, letting in the cool night air.

"Caleb?" She ran to the window and peered out. "CALEB!"

Spinning away from the window, she ran back to the living room. The bathroom door was open, and in the light from her son's room, she could see it was empty. Thrusting her feet into her running shoes, she grabbed her keys and rushed outside.

Brake lights flashed at the end of the road. Fear clawing up her throat, Grace ran with every ounce of speed she possessed to catch up to the car. But it was no use. The vehicle disappeared out of sight in a matter of seconds.

No! Caleb! What was going on? Who had taken her son?

Without hesitation, Grace called 911, her heart beating frantically against her ribs. Her son had been kidnapped!

Who would do this? And why? Her emergency call seemed to take forever to go through, but finally a nice dispatcher answered. "What is your emergency?"

"My six-year-old son was abducted! I live in the Evergreen Court apartment building, please hurry!"

"I'll send detectives to your location. What was your son wearing when you last saw him?"

"Blue Avenger pajamas." Her voice hitched, and tears welled in her eyes. This couldn't be happening. Had the hoodie guy done this? "Please, hurry. Caleb is only six years old! He's scared and alone and helpless . . ." She couldn't go on, thoughts of what might be happening to her sweet little boy were hitting like a truckload of bricks.

Praying wasn't something she did on a regular basis, not since she'd broken things off with Brady Finnegan, but Grace didn't hesitate to throw herself on God's mercy now.

Please, Lord Jesus, please protect my son!

The dispatcher's voice was calm and empathetic, but that didn't make Grace feel any better. She stayed outside, shivering in her thin T-shirt and sleep shorts, as if maybe the car that had taken Caleb away would return him.

It didn't.

Staring at her phone, she reluctantly scrolled through her contacts. The number she had for Brady was seven years old and probably wouldn't work, but she needed to try. Brady was with the FBI. At least she assumed he'd graduated from the academy. Brady was nothing if not determined. Besides, child abductions were usually handled by the federal government, and she desperately needed help.

She needed every single person in law enforcement out there on the street searching for her son!

BRADY'S CELL phone dragged him from sleep. Getting calls in the middle of the night wasn't necessarily unusual, but his eyes widened when he saw Grace's name on the screen.

"Grace? I—uh, is that you?"

"Yes, it's me. Sorry to call so late." There was a hiccuping sound, making him wonder if she was drunk. Why else would she call him all these years after they'd broken up? At midnight, no less.

He swung up into a sitting position, his fingers tightening on the phone. "Is something wrong?"

"Yes, something is terribly wrong." Her voice cracked, and he felt certain she was crying. "My son, Caleb, was kidnapped from his bedroom, and I need your help. Please, Brady, he's only six years old!"

Kidnapped? He rose and reached for his clothes. "Where are you?" Child abductions like this weren't common. Runaways or kids being lured from schools or campgrounds were how most human-trafficking victims were grabbed, but this? Ripping a child out of his bedroom in the middle of the night?

Brady hadn't had a case like this—ever.

"I live in the Evergreen Court apartments in Ravenswood." She sniffled loudly, then added, "The detectives have just arrived to talk to me, but please hurry. I need your help to find him."

"I'm on my way." Ravenswood was roughly a fifteen-minute ride from his condo near the FBI office building. He didn't bother with his normal suit and tie, there wasn't time for that. He did make sure to take his sidearm and credentials, though.

It wasn't until he was driving through the darkness to the Evergreen Court apartment building that the fact that his former girlfriend Grace had a six-year-old son. When she'd broken things off with him two weeks into his FBI training at Quantico, she'd mentioned finding someone else.

During tonight's call, she hadn't mentioned being married. But she could be married, divorced, or separated.

Whatever. He told himself their former relationship didn't matter. A missing kid was always top priority. Especially when snatched from his bedroom in the middle of the night.

Had the boy's father taken him? Maybe. He'd worked a few custody cases where kids were taken by the noncustodial parent. If that was the case, the little boy would likely be found unharmed.

At least, he found himself hoping and praying that would be the outcome.

Unfortunately, he'd seen the worst of what people had done to each other. He couldn't bear the thought of a little boy being hurt. Kids were gifts from God and should be protected at all costs.

Too bad there were far too many who saw them as a source of easy money by selling them to pedophiles.

Not this time, Lord, please? Keep this little boy safe in Your care!

When Brady arrived at the Evergreen Court apartment building, which only sported two evergreen trees, one on each side of the three-story building, he could see a petite woman with dark hair talking to a man and woman who were dressed like detectives. He pulled up to the curb and shot out of the car to join them.

"Who are you?" the older man asked with a frown.

"Special Agent Brady Finnegan with the FBI." He lifted his cred pack so they could see his badge and ID. "And you are?"

"Detective Dale Jackson and this is my partner, Detective Lynn Walker." Jackson frowned. "How did you know about the kidnapping? We're just getting the details now."

"Ms. Ramsey called me. We're old friends." He noted Grace's eyes were red and puffy from crying. "I'm sorry, but I really need you to start at the beginning."

"I-I put Caleb to bed at eight. A muffled cry woke me at midnight, and I thought he was having a nightmare." Fresh tears rolled down her cheeks. "But when I went into his room, he was gone, and the window was open. I rushed outside and saw red taillights from a car driving away. I tried to chase after him . . ." She buried her face in her hands.

"Hey, it's okay. We're going to find your son." He did his best to sound reassuring. The two detectives nodded, although he could see by their expressions there wasn't much to go on. "Let's go inside. We'll need to ask a lot of questions, Grace. It may sound probing, but this is the best way we can find the person responsible."

"I—okay." She glanced at the detectives. "I was just telling them about the guy in a hoodie."

His pulse spiked. "What guy in a hoodie?"

"Ms. Ramsey called the precinct earlier this evening after seeing a man wearing a dark hoodie outside the day care center where she works," Detective Lynn Walker said. "She saw him twice, but apparently, he never stuck around for very long."

"Could this man be your ex?" Brady asked. "Caleb's father?"

"No." Grace vehemently shook her head. "He was a stranger. I've never seen him before. I'm not married. Caleb's dad isn't part of his life."

"Okay, I had to ask." He put a hand on her arm. "Come on, Grace, you're shivering. Let's go inside."

She turned, stumbled a bit, then headed into the building. He and the detectives followed. He frowned when he saw she had a ground-level apartment with the word *Manager* on the door.

"How long have you lived here?"

"Almost six years." She stared blankly at her pullout sleeper sofa, then gestured to the kitchen table. "I—uh, it's a one bedroom. Caleb's room . . ." She didn't finish.

"Let's see it," he said.

Grace paused long enough to pull on a cardigan sweater, then led the way down the very short hall where the bedroom was located. The room was chilly from the open window; the bed covers were in a lump in the middle of the mattress. Crossing to the window, he could see that the entire window and screen had been expertly cut away, enabling the kidnapper to sneak into the room, grab the boy, then escape the same way.

The little boy would have fought, though, wouldn't he? Even at six? Brady didn't have a lot of experience with kids but made a mental note to talk to his fellow agent Marc Callahan about that. Marc had several kids, and his oldest son, Max, was about five or six too.

"Did you touch anything?" Lynn Walker asked.

"The covers, I thought Caleb was having a nightmare. I —didn't realize he was gone until I turned the lights on." Grace buried her face in her hands again.

"Hey, you're helping us find him now." He put an arm around her slim shoulders, briefly remembering their last night together. The night they'd let their emotions cloud their better judgement. "We'll get a team in here to check for fingerprints. Maybe the perp left something behind."

"Okay." She sniffed and used the hem of her sweater to wipe her face. Leaving the bedroom, she paused, then said, "He took Lucy with him."

"Lucy?" Brady scanned the room. "A doll?"

"A stuffed dog. He named her Lucy." Her voice hitched again. "He loves that dog; it's been with him since we moved here."

"That's a good detail to know." Brady followed Grace from the room back to the small kitchenette. It hurt to realize Grace had lived here in Wisconsin for the past six years without once contacting him. Well, until tonight. Sternly reminding himself to stay focused on the missing six-year-old boy, he took a seat at the table along with the detectives. "Add the stuffed dog named Lucy to the Amber Alert. We may want to have Grace work with a sketch artist to get a likeness of the hoodie guy."

"I'll make a note," Walker said. She seemed to be the more junior detective, at least judging by the way she looked younger than her counterpart.

He pulled out the chair and gestured for Grace to join them. "We'll need the names of your family and friends, anyone you can think of who might know something about where Caleb is."

"Why would my family or friends know who took him?" Grace glared at him through red eyes. "They wouldn't have to break into the apartment in the middle of the night. Caleb rides the van from the day care to school and back each day. They could simply meet up with him at school if that was their intent."

"Please, Grace, the more people we can talk to, the better." He understood her concern, but they could not afford to leave any stone unturned. "I seem to remember your parents live in Chicago and you have an older brother? Adam? Is he in Chicago too?"

She nodded, sniffled, then reached for a tissue. "Adam is in Illinois, and I haven't seen him in years. He won't be any help. I haven't seen my parents since Christmas either. They live in Florida now. I don't have a lot of friends, but I'm fairly close with the day care center staff who work for me."

"You own the day care?" He glanced at her in surprise.

"Yes. The Bright Stars day care center." She hesitated, then added, "I have five staff members—four are full time, one is part time."

"Their names?" Lynn Walker held her pencil ready.

"Sarah Brown, Candace Taylor, Stacy Copeland, Joyce Radecki, and Marie Norquist." She hesitated, then added, "Stacy is the oldest of the group. The kids sometimes call her Nanna because her grandson Charlie attends the day care too."

Brady took down each of the employees' names too. The FBI hadn't been officially called in on the case, but that didn't matter. He was going to work it regardless, and it was too bad if his boss didn't like it. He had vacation time coming, he'd work it on his own time if necessary.

"Is Caleb about the same age as Charlie? Do they look similar? Is it possible someone took him by mistake?" he asked.

"Yes. Charlie is six too." Grace straightened in her seat, looking energized for the first time since he'd arrived. "Do you think that's possible?" Then her face fell. "But they should have known Charlie didn't live here. This kidnapper took Caleb out of his bed!"

"It's just a theory," he hastened to explain. "I'm sorry. I

shouldn't be thinking out loud. I'm just trying to understand the dynamics at the Bright Stars day care."

"It's a day care!" Grace didn't bother to hide the frustration in her tone. She surged to her feet. "You need to be out there, looking for him. What if they take him out of the city? Out of the state?" Her eyes widened with panic. "He could end up anywhere!"

"Grace, please, you need to stay calm." He took her hand and tugged her back down. "We can't blindly search for your son. We need to have people to talk to and search for possible witnesses."

Her large green eyes filled with fresh tears. "There wasn't anyone outside when I ran after the car."

"You never know who was looking through their window at any given time." He turned to the pair of detectives. "Do you have officers canvassing the area? Have you put out an Amber Alert?"

"We have issued an Amber Alert," Jackson confirmed. "Ms. Ramsey gave us a photo of the boy in his Avengers pajamas."

The idea of this kid being taken in his pajamas made his gut tighten. The sooner they found this little guy, the better. "Okay, that's good. It may help prevent the kidnapper from getting too far."

"May? Might?" Grace shook her head. "I can't stand it, Brady. I can't stand the idea of Caleb being afraid, or hurt, or . . ."

"Don't do this," he quickly interjected. "Let's not assume the worst. Is there any reason someone may want to get back at you? To take your son out of anger or revenge? Did you take over the day care center from someone else?"

"I bought the day care business from Stacy; she didn't want the hassle of running it." Grace sniffed and blew her nose again. "I don't have any enemies that I'm aware of. None."

"Okay, that's fine. You're doing great." He strove to sound positive, although the interview was not providing them much to go on. Glancing at the detectives, he raised a brow silently asking if they had additional questions.

"Ms. Ramsey, we'd still like to check with your family," Lynn Walker said gently. "Should we start with your parents? Honestly, you shouldn't be alone at a time like this."

"You can call them, Ed and Janice Ramsey. They live in Tampa, Florida."

"What about your brother, Adam?" Brady met her gaze. "Has he gotten married? Have any kids of his own?"

"No." Her gaze darted away from his in a way that made him uneasy. "At least, not that I know of. We don't talk."

"Since when?"

Grace shook her head, still avoiding his gaze. She didn't answer for a long moment, before finally admitting, "Since I left Chicago."

Considering she'd moved here six years ago, he assumed that's how long she'd been out of touch with her brother. He caught Walker's gaze and gave an imperceptible nod. Adam was someone they needed to speak with, and very soon.

Lynn understood what he was saying. She stood and moved away to begin making calls, but Grace abruptly stood.

"Don't bother," she said quickly. "I know you're going to call him, but it won't work. Adam isn't involved in this. That would be completely impossible."

"Why is that?" Brady pressed.

She swung to face him, an agonizing expression crossing her features. "Because he's in federal prison for fraud."

The news stunned him. "What kind of fraud?"

"He embezzled money from an investment scheme. A fake pyramid type of investment fund similar to what Bernie Madoff did." She waved a hand. "What does that matter? Talking to Adam is a dead end. He didn't do this. He wasn't the one outside the day care wearing a hoodie! You need to be out there looking for Caleb!" Her voice wavered. "Please, Brady. Please find him."

"We'll do everything possible," he assured her. "I need a photo of Caleb too. Can you please send it to me?"

There was the slightest pause before she reached for her phone.

His phone pinged, and the image of a small blond six-year-old boy wearing blue Avengers pajamas bloomed on the screen. His breath froze in his throat. He could have been looking at a picture of himself at the same age. The little boy was a mirror image of him.

The timing hit hard, and he tore his gaze from the picture to see a flash of guilt flicker in Grace's green gaze. In that moment, he knew.

Caleb was his son.

CHAPTER TWO

Brady knew the truth. Grace could see it in his eyes. She squelched the flash of guilt and regret. She couldn't change the past and had broken things off for Brady's sake in the first place. Federal agents couldn't associate with criminals, and she was afraid her brother's crimes would ruin his chances of success. Once her brother had finally landed in jail? Yes, she should have come forward. It was why she'd been thinking about doing that very thing earlier. But right now, all that mattered was finding Caleb.

She waited for Brady to say something, but the quick glance he shot toward the detectives made her realize he wanted to have this conversation in private. Was it possible he wouldn't be allowed to work the case if he was Caleb's biological father? She needed everyone in law enforcement to be out searching for him.

Everyone!

"Got it." Detective Lynn lowered the phone and came back to the table. "We're going to check on the brother, who is in prison." When Grace opened her mouth to say I told you so, Lynn lifted a hand and added, "We still need to vet him. Your brother could have hired someone to do this, or maybe one of his disgruntled investors did the deed. It's an avenue we need to pursue."

Grace closed her eyes, feeling sick. "Adam could be seeking revenge," she whispered. "I helped turn him in to the authorities."

"You did?" Brady lifted a brow. "You testified against him?"

"Not exactly." She twisted her fingers together, realizing there was no point in hiding the truth now. "Originally, I sent copies of his emails anonymously to the feds. When it seemed that wouldn't be enough, I broke down and called. It seemed to take forever for them to investigate his company. He was only arrested and charged with fraud in April of last year."

"A little over a year ago." Brady's brown eyes seemed laser focused when they drilled into her. "He knows you did this?"

"I assume so." She shrugged and spread her hands. "The feds had so much evidence against him Adam apparently took a deal rather than take the case to trial. I don't see why my brother would bother to take Caleb, though. For what purpose? Money? That won't do him any good now that he's in prison. What other reason is there?"

"We won't know until we talk to him." Brady looked at his watch with a grimace. "Which we can't do until nine a.m."

"That's hours from now." It was all she could do not to cry and scream at the top of her lungs. All this talking was getting them nowhere. "It's already past one o'clock in the morning. Caleb has been missing for more than an hour." Her heart squeezed painfully in her chest. "Surely there's something you can do to find him."

The detectives stood and moved toward the door. "We'll start canvassing the area, but it is the middle of the night. We may not get very far."

"Doing something is better than nothing." She rose and crossed to the doorway. "Please let me know if you find anything."

"We will," Detective Lynn Walker assured her. Grace felt certain this woman understood better than most what she was going through. Maybe she even had a child of her own.

"Thank you." Grace hadn't meant to sound ungrateful. She wasn't a cop, but obviously they needed clues of some sort to follow up on.

Too bad she had nothing but a guy in a hoodie she'd seen twice.

"How soon can I work with a sketch artist?" She turned to face Brady. "Maybe someone will recognize the hoodie guy."

"Not until morning." He held her gaze. "Why didn't you tell me about Caleb? The only reason I haven't been involved in his life was because I didn't know about him! Don't you think I had the right to know about my son?"

She turned away, wishing they didn't have to do this. "He's missing, Brady. Can we hash this out later and focus on finding him?"

"I plan to follow up on the investors who lost money to your brother, but I still want to know why you kept my son from me?" There was a painful edge to his tone. "I lost years of my son's life because of you, Grace. I loved you. I trusted you. And now I discover you betrayed me in the worst possible way."

A flash of anger had her spinning toward him. "I didn't know I was pregnant until after I broke things off. And I only did that because I discovered what Adam was doing. Don't you understand? I didn't want to jeopardize your career with the bureau."

His expression didn't soften. "You honestly believe I would give up my son for a career with the bureau? You really didn't know me at all, did you?"

"No! I didn't think that. But once I discovered the truth . . ." Her voice trailed off. He was right, she should have called him. "After I sent information to the feds, I left Chicago without telling my brother where I was going. I didn't want him to try to find me. I kept thinking that once he was arrested, the coast would be clear. But it took forever for them to investigate."

"That still doesn't explain why I haven't met my six-year-old son." He sounded so disgusted with her, and really, she didn't blame him. "And what about this guy you said you were seeing?"

"You can hate me all you want, Brady," she said in a low voice. "I did what I thought was best at the time. Neal and I dated briefly, but we were mostly friends, nothing more. It was wrong for me to keep Caleb from you, but I can't go back to change it. All that matters now is finding Caleb."

He raked his hand over his short blond hair and sighed. "You're right about that, Grace. We will find him." He stepped closer. "But know this, I fully intend to be a part of Caleb's life. He's a Finnegan. I will not allow you to keep him from me."

"I understand. Of course, Caleb needs a father."

"Funny you're just figuring that out now," he shot back. Then he lifted a hand. "Never mind, we'll call a truce until we find him."

"Thank you." Tears filled her eyes. "Please, Brady, I can't stand the idea of him being hurt or worse."

"I know." His voice was gentle now. "We'll put our faith in God to watch over him. Do you have those emails you sent the feds?"

"I—uh, sure." It took a moment for her to switch gears from the subject of prayers to her brother's crimes. She rose and went over to grab her laptop. Setting it on the table, she logged in, hyperaware of Brady hovering over her shoulder. She pulled the message up, then turned the screen toward him. "Here, you can have it all. Anything you want."

"Why don't you get some rest?" He didn't take his gaze from the computer. "We're doing everything we can to find Caleb."

Rest? Was he joking? "It would be impossible to sleep. And I really don't feel like we're doing enough to find him."

"I know. Trust me that I want to find my son just as much as you do." He scrolled down through the emails, then glanced up at her. "I can't believe your brother actually put his scheme in writing where it could be discovered."

"Well, to be fair, I overheard a phone call that sparked concern. It was only then that I sneaked in and started going through his emails." The secrets she'd uncovered years ago came rolling back with a vengeance. "I kept thinking there had to be some sort of mistake. Something I didn't understand."

"No, I think it's pretty clear what he was doing," Brady said dryly. "Can you recall anyone in particular who was upset with losing their money?"

"They were all upset." She paused, thinking back. "His biggest fish—as Adam called him, was a man by the name of Arnold Finch. He apparently invested twenty million dollars, moving his entire portfolio from one brokerage account to Adam's company. Adam used Finch to get even more investors while spending large chunks of their money on himself." Even after all these years, she felt sick at how her brother had allowed greed to go to his head.

"Okay, Finch is a good place to start." Brady went back to working on the computer. She couldn't sit still, so she paced the short length of her apartment. Then she went over to straighten the sheets and blanket on her sofa sleeper. After storing that away, she had more room to pace.

Her brain darted from one possibility to the next. Had someone noticed Caleb while at the day care center? One of the parents, or maybe a grandparent? Had he been taken by a stranger or someone she knew?

Why, Lord, why?

"Grace, if you don't get some rest, you won't be any help when it comes to following up on a potential lead." Brady's voice of reason grated like nails raking a chalkboard.

"I can't rest when he's out there alone, scared, hurt, and crying!" Her voice broke, but she managed to pull herself together. "Don't worry about me, just find Caleb."

"I intend to, but Caleb is going to need you to be strong when we find him."

The words washed over her, making her realize he was right. She couldn't be a mess once they found Caleb. She'd need to be there for her son.

For their son.

No, she couldn't deal with the guilt over keeping Caleb a secret from Brady. There would be time for that later. Once her little boy was home, safe and sound.

She dropped onto the sofa and scrubbed her hands over her face. Her eyes were puffy and gritty, her nose a runny mess. Watching Brady work on the computer so calmly irrationally made her want to hit him.

Of course, she didn't. It was just that her emotions were in chaos, partially because she couldn't help thinking the worst. It was a good thing that Brady was deeply committed to uncovering a clue as to where Caleb might be. She had to trust the police process.

She had to trust Brady.

And God.

Rising to her feet, she stumbled toward her son's room. His messy bed and his missing stuffed dog, Lucy.

"Grace?" Instantly, Brady was beside her, his hand on her arm, holding her back. "You can't be in here. We still need the crime scene techs to go through."

She swallowed hard. Was it too much to ask that she take his pillow? Breathe in his baby shampoo scent from his bath? With reluctance, she turned away, stepping into Brady. He pulled her close and smoothed a hand down her back.

"I know this is difficult, but we're doing everything we can." His voice was low and husky in her ear. "Just give us a little time. The crime scene techs will be here soon, okay?"

"Okay." Her voice was muffled against his chest. In that moment, he was the same Brady he'd been seven years ago when they'd shared their passionate night together, the last night before he'd boarded a flight to Virginia.

The arguments they'd had over her secret faded. In that moment, there was just the two of them together, clinging to each other for support.

"I'm so sorry, Brady. I feel terrible you had to find out about Caleb like this." She knew her regret was too little, too late. "I'm glad you're here now, though."

"Me too." He held her for a long moment before stepping back. A knock at the door had her almost tripping over him to reach it. "Probably the techs," he warned, in case she was expecting to see her son standing there.

As Brady deduced, two crime scene techs stood there.

Masking her disappointment, she let them in and let Brady take over with providing instructions on what they should be looking for.

Reminding herself she was grateful for Brady's FBI expertise, she sank back onto the sofa and held herself together with an effort. They would find Caleb. They had to.

She could not lose her son!

BRADY RETURNED to the kitchen table to continue working through the list of names he was compiling from the emails Grace had taken from her brother's computer.

Staying focused on the task at hand helped keep his anger in check. Being upset with Grace for the magnitude of her lie was useless and would not help find Caleb.

Still, it burned to know that once they did find him, the poor kid wouldn't know him. And would likely be afraid of him, especially after his ordeal. All strangers would be scary, and Brady couldn't stand the idea of his own son being frightened by him.

Enough, those thoughts were not helpful either. They had two clues: Adam's investors who'd lost millions of dollars and the hoodie guy Grace had seen lurking nearby. Brady didn't like jumping to conclusions, but it made sense the hoodie guy had been hired by someone else to snatch the boy. Granted, it was possible the investor victim had dressed up in the hoodie to do the job himself, but he doubted it.

If the kidnapper's motive was money, a repayment for the funds he'd lost, Brady prayed Grace would get a ransom demand very soon.

Something she obviously hadn't considered, at least not yet.

He had his list of suspects prioritized by the amount of money they'd lost and how much their current net worth was now by the time the techs finished with Caleb's room. They were able to get some prints off the window frame, but he knew there was a strong possibility they would belong to Caleb or Grace. Then again, not all criminals were smart. And if this one was fueled by anger and revenge, he could have easily slipped up.

Standing in the doorway to Caleb's room, after Grace pulled some clothes from the closet to change into jeans and a short-sleeved top, he took note of the piles of books and toys in one corner. The closet was filled halfway with Grace's clothes and the other half with Caleb's things. He didn't like thinking of her scraping by in a one-bedroom place. If he'd been making child support payments, she could have afforded something better.

And he'd have a bedroom in his condo for Caleb to use too.

He took out his phone and looked at the image of the smiling little boy. His son. Turning away, he focused on the list. Maybe this Finch guy was responsible, but he was more interested in the man who'd invested and lost his entire life savings along with his house after his wife divorced him.

Paul Moore had nothing to lose by kidnapping Caleb and everything to gain. Or at least, that was likely his thought process. Brady pulled up pictures of his three top suspects, then turned to Grace. "Come and look at these men, see if anything about them looks familiar."

Grace lifted her head from the arm of the sofa, then rolled to her feet. She staggered a bit, as if she'd just woken up. He reached for her hand to steady her.

"Thank you." Her fingers were icy cold, and he belatedly realized the open window in Caleb's room had brought the temperature down in the small apartment. He made a note to have someone come and board up the window in the morning.

Grace pulled her chair close to the computer so she could peer at the screen. To her credit, she took her time, looking at each of the three men intently. Finally, her shoulders slumped, and she shook her head. "I'm sorry. I've never seen these three men before in my life."

"Not even on the news after your brother's crimes were exposed?" He stared at her, silently urging her to remember. "There's an article here that says each of these men were questioned by the Chicago FBI office. Surely you remember hearing about this on the news."

"I didn't watch the news." She turned from the computer. "Do you think it's easy to know your brother stole millions of dollars for his own use? Why do you think I left Chicago to come to Ravenswood? Because I wanted to raise my son in a quiet place, out of the spotlight, and away from those who might hold us responsible."

"Your son?" The sharp question slipped out before he could stop it.

"Our son." She winced and shook her head. "I've already apologized. What happened to that truce you promised?"

He hated having his words tossed back at him. Something each of his eight siblings loved to do. "Okay, you're right about the truce. I need to be sure you absolutely have not seen either of these men before Caleb went missing."

"I have not." She hunched her shoulders. "Do you think one of them is cruel or desperate enough to have kidnapped Caleb?"

"I think they have a strong motivation to get money back from the man who ripped them off. And since Adam is in jail, that leaves you."

"Okay, but what do they expect me to do? Get their money back for them? That's impossible. Whatever Adam didn't spend was returned to the investors. Granted, it was a pittance to what they'd lost, but it was something."

"I know, but they might think your brother has money stashed in a safe place or, more likely, in offshore accounts."

She narrowed her gaze. "Are you saying the feds may not have found all the money?"

"I'm saying the kidnapper may believe the feds have not found all the money," he corrected. "And if that is the motive, you'll receive a ransom call. Possibly later this morning, once the banks are open."

Her jaw dropped. "But I don't have any money! And I also don't have access to any of Adam's illegal funds!"

"I know, we'll deal with that once we get the call." He thought briefly about his sister Kyleigh's new husband, Bax Scala. Bax had apparently received a fat seven-figure inheritance from his grandparents' estate. Other than purchasing his very nice condo, he'd given much of it to various charities. Bax might be able to mobilize enough cash to arrange a swap for Caleb. Especially since Brady had no intention of letting the kidnapper get away with the ransom.

Again, that was a problem to be worked out later. He wouldn't bother Kyleigh about that yet. She wouldn't be thrilled about asking her new husband for that sort of favor anyway. He also knew the entire Finnegan family would pull as many of their assets together to fund an exchange too, but that would take time.

Time they didn't have.

His phone rang, startling Grace. Seeing Detective Dale

Jackson's number on the screen, he quickly answered. "Detective? Do you have something?"

"We have one man who happened to be looking outside when a four-door sedan drove away around midnight. He saw Ms. Ramsey come rushing outside too and thought that was strange. He figured maybe she'd had a lover's spat, but when we told him that her son was kidnapped, he quickly described everything he remembered."

"A dark four-door sedan," Brady repeated for Grace's benefit. Her eyes lit up with hope. "Anything more specific? Make or model?"

"He thinks it was a Honda because of the *H* on the back. But he said it was too dark to identify the vehicle's color or the license plate. He thinks it was black but could be a dark gray, green, or blue too."

"A four-door Honda sedan is helpful, thanks, Jackson." He held Grace's gaze. "Go ahead and add that to the Amber Alert too."

"Yeah, we did. Between the car, the kid's photograph, and the stuffed dog, maybe someone will recognize him," Jackson agreed.

"I hope so. Oh, you should know the crime scene techs are processing the fingerprints. If we get a hit, I'll let you know."

"We should be so lucky," Jackson groused.

"I hear you." He glanced at his watch. It was going on three in the morning now, and there wasn't much more they could do. "You've finished the canvass?"

"For now, but we'll have officers hit the area again in the morning. I'm surprised we were able to get even a handful of people to open their door at this hour."

The kidnapping happening at midnight was strange. Especially if the motive was money in exchange for the child. Why risk keeping Caleb safe and calm all night, knowing you couldn't possibly get any money until the morning? Brady hoped this was an indication that the kidnapper would make other mistakes along the way.

"Anything else?" Jackson asked. "Lynn and I are heading back to the precinct unless you want us at the apartment for some reason."

"No, that's all for now. Oh, I'll shoot you my list of fraud victims. That may be another place to start. I'll take the first three, you two can dig into the others."

"Roger that." Jackson disconnected from the line.

"Someone saw a Honda?" Grace grabbed the information like a lifeline.

"Yes, a man on the third floor said he saw a Honda driving by. He also saw you running out into the street as if to catch it."

"That must be Leon Cromwell. He's a sweet man. Did he see anything else? Caleb? Did it look like Caleb was okay?" She grabbed his arm in a tight grip. "Tell me everything. Don't hold back."

"I've told you everything Jackson relayed to me," he assured her. "The witness only saw the car, and he only noticed it because you went running outside after it. He thought you had a fight with your boyfriend. We think it's a Honda, but you should know that sometimes witnesses get details wrong."

"Okay, you're right. But Leon is a good guy, and I trust what he said he saw." She turned and paced the length of the room again. "Is there a tip line set up with the Amber Alert? Has anyone called in yet with news?"

"No, and keep in mind, witnesses that are up and about in the middle of the night are rare. Most people are asleep."

She swallowed hard and nodded. "I know you're right. I

was asleep too. I wish I'd been sleeping with Caleb, then he wouldn't have been taken."

"Don't go down the path of what-if scenarios," he cautioned. "That's a dead end, Grace. Let's stay focused on the present." It struck him that he needed to heed the same advice. To be honest, he'd been so hurt after Grace had broken things off, claiming she'd found someone else, he hadn't bothered to track her down. Despite knowing how they'd been intimate. If he had gone to see her once he'd finished with his training at Quantico, he'd have discovered the truth about his son well before now.

"Yeah, okay." She paced again, then abruptly turned to face him. "I don't have a car, but you do. Couldn't we drive out on the path I last saw the taillights? Maybe see if there isn't a motel or something close by that we can check out?"

It wasn't the worst idea, and it would give her something to do, but he also hated to get her hopes up that finding Caleb would be that easy. "We can try, but try to understand it's not likely the kidnapper would have stopped so close to your apartment. He or she would want distance between you."

"You said yourself criminals aren't always smart," she protested.

"That's true, but we have no idea who we are dealing with. We don't know for sure that money is the motive behind the kidnapping."

The light in her green eyes dimmed, making him feel like a jerk. "Please, Brady. I can't sit here doing nothing for a minute longer."

"Okay, we'll head out for a short drive." A change of scenery couldn't hurt. But then he hesitated. "If Caleb were to get free, does he know his way back here?"

"He's only six, Brady. He knows how to get from our

apartment to the day care center and the grocery store. That's all. If he's far away . . ." She shook her head helplessly. "He wouldn't know how to get back. I hope and pray someone sees him and helps to bring him home."

He nodded, feeling foolish for not knowing what six-year-olds could and couldn't do. His experience with kids was from years back, when the twins were born, followed a few years later by Elly, the oops baby. Frankly, he didn't remember much about that chaotic time.

"Let's go." He led the way as they walked outside to where he'd left his SUV.

"Head that way." Grace gestured with her hand once they were seated. "I think that's south, right?"

"Yes." He fired up the engine and pulled away from the curb. They drove in silence for long moments as he continued on the road where the four-door sedan was last seen. "How long did you follow it?"

"I think about here." She pointed to the intersection up ahead. "The taillights disappeared, and I couldn't tell which way the car turned."

"We'll take both ways for a short distance, see if we find anything." It couldn't hurt to patrol the area, not that he expected to find anything.

Grace was silent, peering out her passenger-side window as if her life depended on it. He scanned the area off to his side, too, while keeping an eye on the road. After ten miles, he was about to turn around when Grace reached over to grab his arm. "Brady? Do you see that?"

"What?" He craned his neck to see where she was pointing. There was something lying on the ground in a parking lot outside a small motel. His heart thudded painfully when he saw a stuffed animal.

Cranking the wheel hard, he went straight toward it. As

they came closer, Grace let out a low tortured moan. "It's Lucy. That's Caleb's stuffed dog, Lucy." She began to sob. "Now he doesn't have anything to comfort him."

"Hold on, Grace. This could be the break we need." He hit the phone on his dash to call Jackson. "Meet us at the Hollow Inn Motel ASAP. And bring backup. The boy might be here."

Grace turned to face him. "You think so?"

"There's only one way to find out." He pulled off to the side so as not to disturb the area, hoping and praying Caleb was being held in one of those rooms.

And that they'd find him safe and unharmed.

CHAPTER THREE

He'd lost his Lucy. Caleb sniffed and rubbed at his eyes, his lower lip quivering. The man had been watching TV, then suddenly jumped up, saying they had to go. He'd lifted Caleb off the bed and rushed out to the car. He'd been so surprised he'd lost his grip on Lucy. Then they were driving away.

After the man had crawled into his window, he'd given Caleb candy to keep him quiet. But now Caleb was tired and wanted his mom. The man kept telling him he'd see his mom soon, but Caleb wasn't sure if he should believe him. Adults always said we'd do something *soon*. Which almost always meant never.

He hoped this man was telling the truth. That he'd see his mom again soon. He didn't like this game of hide-and-seek. The man said it would be fun, but he wasn't having fun anymore. The way they'd left the small room so quickly made him think his mom had been about to find them, but now she couldn't. It was as if the man really didn't want his mom to find them. When the man offered him more candy, he'd shaken his head. He didn't want candy.

He wanted his mom. He wanted to go home.

Caleb started to cry, and the man told him to shut up. He'd cried and cried over losing Lucy, but then he couldn't cry anymore. Maybe his tears had all been used up. His eyelids drifted closed, and he fell asleep.

He dreamed his mom was running toward him, sweeping him into her arms, and hugging him close.

And he smiled.

GRACE COULDN'T HOLD back the fresh tears. The small bit of comfort Caleb had with him was lying in the parking lot. Had the kidnapper ripped it from her son's arms and tossed it aside as some sort of punishment? She lowered her face into her hands, squeezing her eyes shut to avoid imagining the worst.

"I need you to sit tight, Grace. We're going to have this place surrounded in less than two minutes."

"Okay." It wasn't easy to stay away from the motel, she wanted to run inside and demand to see her son. Yet the thought of Brady and the police finding Caleb in one of the rooms was enough to keep her from losing it completely. The stuffed dog meant her son was here. Or had been here. Preferably the former. She drew in several deep breaths and wiped her face with the hem of her sweater. "I want to know the minute you find him, Brady."

"You will, I promise." He held her gaze. "Stay strong, Caleb needs you."

"Yes." She straightened in the passenger seat, knowing he was right. "I'm okay. Just find him."

"That's the goal." When the first few squads arrived and pulled up behind them, Brady quickly pushed out of the SUV. He flashed a reassuring smile, then closed the door and went over to join the officers.

Even at this hour, the place was suddenly lit up like fireworks on the Fourth of July. Grace watched as the officers approached Caleb's stuffed dog, placing a tiny marker near it. Then they headed inside the building as even more police squads arrived.

Some officers began stringing tape across the entrance to the parking lot. It took a moment for her to realize they were treating the entire area as a crime scene.

A crime scene!

Gasping in horror, she stared as more officers arrived. Did they think they were going to find her son in one of these rooms? Injured or worse, dead?

No please, Lord Jesus. Hold my son safe in Your loving arms. Protect him and keep him safe!

Less than a minute later, Brady and the officers came out from the lobby area and approached one of the rooms, one with a number 6 on the door. Grace leaned forward, holding her breath. Brady used the key to access the room, then he ran in, his gun raised. The cop followed right behind him.

Her heart thudded painfully against her breast as the seconds passed with excruciating slowness. Then Brady and the officer came back out. Brady glanced over to her and shook his head, indicating the room was empty.

No! Caleb! She wanted to scream and cry in frustration but managed to hold it together, her gaze glued to the scene before her. More officers trotted over to the motel room door and began stretching more crime scene tape across the opening.

Her heart lodged in her throat. Frantic, she pushed at

the car door, almost falling to the ground in her haste to get out. Brady saw her and quickly ran forward.

"Easy, Grace, there's no sign of an injury. We're just preserving the evidence until the crime scene techs can get here."

"Evidence?" She gripped his jacket. "What kind of evidence?"

"DNA for starters. The bathroom looks used, so we may find trace DNA in the shower and sink. Also, the bed linens will be taken in and searched for skin cells." He pulled her close. "Thanks to finding Lucy, we know Caleb was here, and we'll find the man who took him. He made his first mistake choosing to stay in place so close to your apartment building."

"No blood? You're sure there's no blood?"

"There is no blood." His voice was confident, and she found herself relaxing just enough to rest her forehead on his chest. "The clerk says the man checked in alone. He had no idea the guy was part of the Amber Alert. If he'd have seen a kid, he would have called it in."

She let out her breath in a sigh, desperately wanting to believe that no blood meant that Caleb hadn't been hurt. Then she lifted her head. "Can he give you a description?"

Brady grimaced. "He said the perp was definitely male and in his midthirties. He was wearing a baseball cap, but the clerk thought his hair was dark brown or black. We'll have the clerk work with a forensic sketch artist too."

"So it really was the hoodie guy who took him," she murmured.

"We don't know that the two men are one and the same," Brady cautioned. "Best to follow the facts rather than jumping to conclusions."

Logically he was right, but a flash of annoyance hit hard. Easy for him to say, it wasn't his son missing!

Except, of course, it was.

She glanced over to the middle of the parking lot. "Can I take Lucy? Or do you need the stuffed dog for evidence too?"

"You can take him . . . wait a minute." Brady abruptly let her go. She swayed, missing his solid and reassuring strength. "I need to call Marc Callahan."

"Who?" The name wasn't familiar.

"One of my FBI colleagues. He has a brother Matt who is a K-9 cop, partnered with a German shepherd named Duchess. I wonder if the dog can pick up Caleb's scent and assist us in finding him."

A flicker of hope bloomed in her chest. But then she frowned. "I don't think the K-9 will be able to track him if he was taken by car."

"Maybe not, but we need all the help we can get." Brady turned away. "Marc? It's Brady. Sorry to bother you this early, but we have a missing kid, and I would love some help from your brother Matt and his K-9, Duchess."

Grace couldn't hear the other side of the conversation but could tell by Brady's satisfied expression that Marc was going along with the plan. She told herself that every little bit counts. There was no denying Brady was pulling out every resource he had to find their son.

Turning, her gaze landed on Lucy. Proof that her son had been here, and recently. He'd been taken at midnight, and it was going on four in the morning now.

Four hours. She shivered and wrapped her arms around her chest to keep warm. Four hours and they had no idea where to search next.

Another motel? Maybe one farther away? Or would the

kidnapper avoid public places now that the Amber Alert had gone out?

But if not a motel, then where? Her mind couldn't seem to come up with a single coherent thought.

"Matt and Duchess will be here soon," Brady said. "We'll have the K-9 search the entire area, see if the boy had been anywhere else other than the room. Maybe the kidnapper parked his car somewhere else."

"Does the motel have cameras?"

"No, they don't." Brady scowled. "This place is as low budget as you get. Which is another clue. It could be this kidnapper doesn't have a lot of cash."

She appreciated his positive outlook on these small details, but all they did was make her want to scream in frustration. "If he doesn't have money, then why hasn't he called to demand a ransom?"

"I don't know, but it's something we're preparing for."

"I'll give him all the money I have," she said. Then she realized that would not be enough. She wasn't rich, and if this kidnapping was a way to get back at her brother, the kidnapper would want his retirement fund replenished in full.

Her stomach tightened at the seemingly insurmountable problem. She doubted Brady had enough money for that too. He likely had more than she did, but that wouldn't be enough.

What if they couldn't scrape together the amount needed to pay the ransom demand? Would this kidnapper retaliate by killing a six-year-old boy? No, she couldn't bear it. If the kidnapper was desperate, surely he'd take whatever money they had to offer.

Caleb didn't deserve this. He was only a little boy! She

hadn't cheated anyone out of their life savings. And Caleb shouldn't be held responsible for his uncle's crimes.

Brady rested his hand on her arm, breaking into her depressing thoughts. "I can tell you're already thinking the worst, Grace. Please don't. The only way we'll get through this is by staying positive. By working every single angle of the case. Don't forget, we're going to get this guy's DNA. I'm sure that will be the first step in finding him." Brady paused, then added, "And I know God is watching over our son. We must trust in Him. And in His strength. With God's help, we will find him."

"I know." She truly believed Brady was dedicated in his mission to find Caleb. He'd done nothing but work with her since the moment she'd called him. And she found some comfort in believing God was watching over their little boy.

Still, she couldn't completely erase the doubts that insidiously crept into her mind. She needed to hope and pray Brady's efforts wouldn't be too little, too late.

THE OFFICERS WERE DOING a good job of preserving the scene in a slow, methodical way, but Brady was itching to get moving. Patience wasn't his strong suit. He knew the process took time, especially if the evidence was to be collected and preserved without becoming contaminated, but he wanted those DNA and fingerprint samples now! And the results put through the FBI database.

Granted, the kidnapper may not have a criminal record. In fact, it was more likely this was some angry investor lashing out against Grace because of her brother's scam. Still, they had to try. Especially if the kidnapper was hired to do the deed. Most law-abiding citizens didn't abruptly agree to kidnap a kid for cash.

Thankfully, Marc Callahan had agreed to come and bring his brother Matt and Duchess too. The stuffed dog would be a great scent source, especially if Caleb had been sleeping with it each night. He wasn't sure if Duchess would be able to track the boy, but he had a wild idea of stopping at every motel in the area with the K-9 to see if they could locate Caleb.

It wasn't easy for him to let go of his anger toward Grace over keeping his son a secret for so long. Yet he was very glad she'd called him for help once the boy had been taken. If she hadn't? He still wouldn't know he'd fathered a son. Well, until he'd seen the Amber Alert. Yet her fear and anxiety tugged at his heart. He knew she was suffering over this, and piling on wouldn't help.

Besides, it was better for all of them if he stayed focused on the task at hand. He made a list in his mind. Collect and run the evidence. Have both Grace and the motel clerk meet with the sketch artist to create a likeness of their UNSUB, also known as unknown subject. They'd see if Duchess could pick up Caleb's scent at other locations.

And they'd continue waiting for the inevitable ransom demand.

Money seemed the most likely motive for the kidnapping. He felt certain the Amber Alert had spooked their guy into leaving the motel. Raking his gaze over the scene, he hoped he wasn't missing something.

The sooner he could get Grace and the motel clerk to work with a forensic artist the better. Once they had that image to go with Caleb's photo, he felt certain someone would recognize them.

This perp couldn't hide forever.

MIDNIGHT ABDUCTION   39

Two SUVs rolled up. He recognized his fellow agent Marc Callahan and could see the K-9 logo on the other vehicle. He took Grace's hand. "I'd like you to meet the Callahan brothers."

"Hey, Finnegan," Marc said, giving Grace a solemn nod. "You must be Ms. Ramsey. As a father of three, I can't imagine what you're going through."

"I—thank you," Grace said, her expression grim. "It's the worst day of my life."

"Of course it is," Marc agreed somberly. "But we are going to find Caleb."

Matt came around from the rear of the SUV with a beautiful German shepherd on leash. Brady stayed where he was, unsure of how to approach the fierce-looking dog. "You must be Matt Callahan. I'm Brady Finnegan, and this is Grace Ramsey. It's her son that is missing."

"I've heard so much about the Finnegan family, it's great to meet you." Matt's smile vanished. "I only wish we were meeting under better circumstances. This is Duchess. Duchess, friends." Matt reached over to put a hand on Grace's arm and then did the same with Brady. "Friends, Duch. Friends."

The large dog sniffed at their feet, then wagged her tail. Brady gestured to the stuffed dog lying in the parking lot. "That's Caleb's favorite stuffed animal. I thought it would be a good scent source for Duchess."

"You are right about that." Matt pulled a bag from his pocket. "I'll need to place the toy in here."

"Okay." Brady led the way over.

Matt turned the bag inside out, using it as a glove to pick up the toy. Then he pulled the edges of the bag around it so that the stuffed dog was inside. He held the open bag for Duchess. "This is Caleb. Caleb. Seek Caleb!"

Duchess pushed her nose into the bag, sniffing for a long time. Then her tail wagged as she excitedly whirled away to go to work. Brady had seen K-9 cops in action before, and he was impressed by the way Matt and Duchess worked together. They were clearly an amazing team.

The dog made a zigzag pattern, heading in the general direction of the motel room. He heard Grace gasp as the dog let out a sharp bark and sat right near the door labeled room 6.

"That's her alert," Marc said with satisfaction. "Duchess is letting us know the boy was inside."

"That's good." It was something they'd already suspected, but the K-9's alert confirmed it. "I'd like them to search the entire area outside the motel. It could be they walked to that gas station for a few things." He gestured to the gas station/convenience store that was barely twenty yards away.

"Matt knows the drill," Marc said confidently. "Let's give him and Duchess time to work the area."

"Of course. That is why I called you." He reminded himself that the police process takes time and struggled to remain patient. He noticed Grace's gaze was locked on the K-9 cop. Matt took Duchess inside the room for several minutes, before returning to the parking lot. Even from here, he could hear Matt giving Duchess instructions. "Seek! Seek Caleb!"

The dog lifted her nose, sniffing the air. She trotted back to where the stuffed animal was, but then turned toward the gas station. Brady held his breath, praying the K-9 would find out that the boy had been there.

But Duchess didn't alert. She sniffed the ground, the air, and made several zigzag paths, but then came to stand beside Matt.

"Well, she hasn't picked up the scent at the gas station," Marc said. "But that doesn't mean our UNSUB didn't stop in there. Let's see if they have any cameras."

"May I come with you?" Grace asked. "I called my lead staff member at the day care center to let her know I wouldn't be in today. I want to stay with you as we work the case. I promise I won't get in the way. Please, I need to do this."

"Sure." He didn't see the harm in allowing her to tag along. Marc glanced at him curiously but didn't comment. Matt and Duchess joined them.

"She alerted all over the motel room," Matt said. "I think she has his scent now, so if we get another lead, she'll be ready to go."

"I was hoping you'd be willing to stop at a few more motels in the area, see if she can pick up his scent." Brady held Matt's gaze. "I know that's asking a lot. But it's the only clue we have."

"We can do that," Matt readily agreed. "Give me your phone number. If Duchess alerts on anything, I'll call."

"Thanks." Brady gave him his information and Grace's too. Matt and Duchess veered off to their SUV, while they continued to the gas station. The hour was closer to five o'clock in the morning now, and he could see someone unlocking the door of the gas station and heading inside. The hours on the door indicated the station closed at midnight. If the perp had come here, it was prior to when he'd snatched Caleb.

A quick conversation with the owner, Albert Cohen confirmed that the camera outside had been broken for the past four months and that he hadn't worked the late shift.

"Do you remember a man wearing a hoodie or a base-ball hat coming in at all?" Brady asked.

Cohen scoffed. "I had lots of customers, many with hoodies or wearing ball caps. I don't remember anyone acting weird or suspicious if that's what you're asking."

"Have you seen the Amber Alert that went out about a missing six-year-old boy wearing Avengers pajamas?" Brady drilled a stern look into Albert's eyes. "Think back again. This is important."

"Yeah, I heard about it on my way in." Albert looked chagrined. "I honestly don't remember any man coming in with a kid that fits that description. If I did, I'd have called you guys right away. But so many people pass by here, it would be impossible for me to tell you if I saw your guy without something more to go on."

"Okay." Brady suppressed a sigh. "Thanks for your help. We may have a sketch I'll need you to look at later."

"I can do that." Albert suddenly seemed eager to please. "You want to talk to my second-shift guy? Trent will be here at five."

"Sure, that would be great, thanks." Brady turned away, hating to admit the gas station was a bust.

"I can check back here later to talk to Trent," Marc offered.

"Twelve hours from now? That's fine, but see if you can't get him up earlier. I don't want to wait twelve hours, I'm hoping and praying we have Caleb back by then." Brady glanced at Grace's pale features, knowing she was feeling just as dejected as he was. "Once we get the sketch, we can return to canvass the area. Maybe Duchess will come up with something. Or we'll get a hit on the prints and DNA from the room. This guy isn't that far ahead of us. If Grace hadn't noticed the stuffed dog, we wouldn't even be here."

"I told you that going out to look for him was better than

sitting in the apartment." She sighed and asked, "So what now? I feel like we need to do more."

He shared her frustration. "I'll find out what the timeline is for the sketch artist. That may help us nail his movements leading up to or after the abduction."

"We only want to know where he is now!" There was an edge to Grace's tone. "If this is about money, why hasn't he called?"

"It could be he's busy finding another place to hide out," Marc pointed out. "And he knows the banks don't open until nine o'clock. Calling earlier isn't going to help him. Just the opposite."

"Yes, he'll know that the moment he makes contact we'll double down on finding him. Which reminds me." He turned to Marc. "We need that tap set up on Grace's cell phone."

"It's being set up right now." Marc glanced at his watch. "I'll check in on the sketch artist too."

"Thanks." He glanced around the area, knowing there was nothing more to do there. "We may as well grab something to eat."

"I can't eat," Grace said. "Can't we just please do something?"

"We are, Grace." He tried to sound reassuring. "We're working the case. As soon as the sketch artist is ready, we'll get you connected with her. The motel clerk too."

"Hey, Agent Finnegan?" Brady turned when he heard his name. The sergeant on scene held up his phone. "My boss wants to talk to you."

"Thanks." He hurried over to take the sergeant's cell phone. "This is Agent Finnegan."

"This is Lieutenant Yale. We're starting to get some calls on the tip line about your Amber Alert. I have officers following up, but we may need more resources from the bureau as the day goes on."

"Yeah, that's fine. I'll get more people on this." Brady was surprised they'd gotten any calls at this early hour. "Do you have anything promising?"

"Not really, but as I said, I have officers making return calls to get more information."

"Okay, I appreciate everything you're doing, Lieutenant. I would like to be notified if the lab gets any hits on the fingerprints lifted from the scene."

"I just checked with them; they have several decent prints that we're running through the system now. We haven't gotten any hits yet." Lieutenant Yale hesitated, then added, "We did get several child-sized prints too, confirming the boy was in there."

"I know, we have a K-9 cop here who alerted on the boy's scent too." The news that had sparked hope just an hour ago was no comfort now. "The DNA will take longer, but I've asked them to put a rush on it. A boy's life is on the line, so they agreed."

"Good, I'm glad to hear it." Lieutenant Yale sighed. "It's never easy when kids are involved."

"No, it's not." Brady disconnected from the call and handed the phone back to the sergeant. He hadn't mentioned that the child in danger was also his son. A fact he'd kept secret from Marc Callahan too. He didn't like keeping things from his friends, and after the past few months of working cases with Marc, he considered the guy to be a friend more so than a coworker. Yet telling the truth would put an end to his involvement in the case. Besides, the connection wasn't pertinent to the investigation. He didn't think his being Caleb's biological father had anything to do with his disappearance.

How could it? He hadn't even known the truth himself. The Finnegans were a close-knit family, more so because of the way they'd hung together after their parents died ten years ago. His oldest brothers, Rhy and Tarin, had moved back home to help take care of the youngest siblings. The twins, Aiden and Alanna, had been seventeen and Elly, the youngest, only fourteen at the time. Brady had been off at college and then had headed to the FBI academy in Quantico, so he hadn't been able to help as much. He'd done whatever he could, but there was no denying Rhy and Tarin had taken the brunt of the responsibility.

Yet if his siblings had known about Grace being pregnant with his child, they would have welcomed her and the baby with open arms.

"Brady?" Grace's urgent voice broke into his thoughts. "I have a call from an unknown number!"

"Marc, get the wiretap going!" He raced over to Grace, dragging her toward the privacy of the SUV. He didn't want any background noise to clue the kidnapper in on how close they were on his tail.

He mentally kicked himself for not being better prepared. It wasn't logical that the kidnapper would call this early. Yet maybe this was what they needed to break the case wide open.

"He's gone! The kidnapper just disconnected!" Grace's stricken features hit him square between his eyes. "What now?"

His stomach churned as a wave of guilt washed over him. He couldn't bear the thought of failing in the biggest mission of his life.

He just couldn't!

CHAPTER FOUR

It wasn't Brady's fault, but Grace had to use every ounce of willpower she possessed not to throw her phone at him. The next time the kidnapper called, she would answer immediately, whether Brady's team was ready or not. She wanted, needed to hear her son's voice. To know Caleb was okay.

Deep down, she also knew Brady was her best chance of getting Caleb back safely. It was why she'd called him. Still, the lost connection hit hard. Her knees buckled under the weight of despair.

"Hey, it's okay. We're going to find him." Brady was instantly at her side, wrapping his strong arm around her waist and helping her into the SUV. "This guy is going to call again. Especially if he wants money."

"Money." It made her sick to her stomach to think of the outrageous ransom demand the kidnapper would likely ask for. She swiped at the tears in her eyes. "It's inconceivable that anyone would terrorize a child for money."

"Trust me, this guy is an amateur, someone looking to get his investments back. He won't hurt Caleb. His focus will be on getting the cash." Brady's voice sounded so certain she couldn't help glancing up at him.

"How do you know he's an amateur?"

"He's made several mistakes. Taking the kid in the middle of the night, which forces him to hold Caleb somewhere safe until the banks open. He also ran off from the motel, probably after seeing the Amber Alert, rather than staying put."

Maybe the kidnapper had made mistakes, but they were still no closer to finding him.

"He'll call back," Brady repeated. "I'm sure of it. But that does raise a question. How would he get your number?"

"It's on my day care website." She thought back to the hoodie guy who had been lurking around hours before Caleb had been taken. "That's the only place I have it listed. Oh, and I had a weird prank call earlier in the evening. I blocked the number." She wanted to hit something. "That must have been the kidnapper. Although how could he call again if I blocked his number?"

"It would make sense that he would test the number to make sure you answered, probably using a different phone." Brady held her gaze for a long moment. "We'll head to the local precinct soon so you and the clerk can work with a sketch artist."

"That's fine. The sooner the better." Having a job to do was a good distraction. Especially if the sketch would help bring Caleb home.

"Why don't you head to the precinct now?" Marc suggested. "I know the kidnapper will call again, but in the meantime, we need to keep the wheels of the investigation churning. I can keep an eye on things here."

Brady hesitated, obviously torn. "Okay. That works. Thanks, Marc."

"Anytime." Marc eyed Brady curiously, making Grace wonder if he sensed the relationship between her and Brady went back further in time. Years before tonight.

"Call me if you get anything off the canvass." Brady stepped back from the SUV and closed her door. She sank into the seat cushion, fatigue washing over her. It seemed wrong to be tired when Caleb was missing. As if her body shouldn't let her down when she needed every ounce of her strength to keep going.

To keep searching.

The roller coaster of emotions was wearying. As Brady slid in behind the wheel, she straightened in her seat and did her best to look alert. "Matt is taking Duchess around to other motels, right?"

"He is, yes. And he's available if we need him for something else."

"Good. I have a lot of faith in Duchess's tracking ability." She twisted her fingers in her lap. "Just watching the dog work was amazing."

"I agree. Matt and Duchess are a good team." He glanced at her. "I'm sorry I let you down."

"You didn't." Had her feelings been so clearly etched on her face? She sighed, then added, "I was upset, but I know it's not your fault the kidnapper disconnected from the call. But I can't help but wonder if he knew we might be trying to trace him."

"You may be right. If so, he may try several short calls to avoid that." Brady reached over to take her hand. "The most important part of the ransom call is to insist on talking to Caleb. To have him tell you something only he would know."

"I will." She would have given anything to hear her son's voice right at that moment. "I'm assuming the FBI will come up with the money to use in an exchange?"

"That's possible." She frowned at the slightest bit of hesitation in his tone. "If not, I have an alternate plan. Either way, we'll make the exchange. Nothing is more important than Caleb."

"Thank you." She tightened her fingers around his. "I truly would be lost without you, Brady."

"We're in this together," he agreed. His fingers were warm around hers. "And I'm not going to rest until we have him."

She stared at their joined hands, wondering how different her life would have been if she'd broken down and called Brady when she'd discovered she was pregnant with Caleb. At the time, she'd told herself his career was more important, but now?

If she'd have called Brady seven years ago, would Caleb have been kidnapped out of a first-floor apartment by one of her brother's victims? She highly doubted it.

This was her fault. Not that she'd intentionally put her son in harm's way, but her decision seven years ago had sent her down this path. The one where she'd convinced herself she'd taken the high road.

Yet she was forced to admit she'd taken the coward's way out. She'd been afraid to tell Brady about their son. Afraid of what would happen to his career and, more importantly, what might happen to her. They hadn't been engaged to be married; he'd never made any promises for the future. In part because new FBI agents didn't get to pick their office location. Their assignments were issued on an as needed basis. She'd also been afraid that Brady would fight for custody.

No, she'd known with absolute certainty he would have fought for custody.

And would have possibly gotten full custody based on her brother's criminal background.

"I know this isn't the time, but once we have Caleb home safe, I'd like to talk to you about how we'll manage things moving forward." Brady spoke as if he'd read her mind. "I want to be a part of my son's life."

"I know. I'm sure we'll come up with something." She kept her response vague because she wasn't ready to think about nights and weekends where she would be sitting home alone while Caleb spent time with Brady.

Not just Brady, but likely his entire family.

The thought should have been reassuring, but the ache in her chest worsened.

The ride to the precinct didn't take long. She'd never been inside a police station. Even after her brother was arrested, they'd interviewed her in her house. There were cubicles and desks scattered around, most of them empty because of the early hour.

"Lieutenant Yale?" Brady moved forward to shake an officer's hand. "Special Agent Brady Finnegan and this is Grace Ramsey, the child's mother."

"Ms. Ramsey." Lieutenant Yale gave her a solemn nod. "Bethany Shear, our forensic sketch artist, will be here soon. I can offer you some coffee; I just made a fresh pot."

"That would be great, thanks." Maybe the kick of caffeine would help give her a badly needed boost of energy.

"Make that two, please," Brady said. "Anywhere in particular you'd like us to sit?"

"This desk up front is fine. The day shift won't be in for

another hour or so." Yale went over to fill two mugs with coffee.

"As soon as Bethany gets here, I'm going to run back and pick up the motel clerk," Brady said as he accepted his cup of coffee. "I want him to work with her too."

She grabbed his arm. "You're leaving me alone? What if the kidnapper calls?"

He covered her hand with his and nodded. "You make a good point. I'll arrange for the clerk to be brought here by one of the other officers."

"Thank you." She abruptly pulled out her phone. "I have half my battery left but will need to recharge it soon."

"We have the same type of phone. I have a connector in the car." He smiled gently. "I'll grab it now so we can charge your phone while we're here."

"Okay." It was completely illogical, but she didn't want him to leave her alone. She wasn't the one in danger, Caleb was. And sitting in the police station was the safest place to be. When Brady stood and walked away, it was all she could do not to run after him.

Ridiculous to feel lost without him sitting beside her. Especially since he hadn't been a part of her life in the past seven years. She stood and crossed to the coffeepot to add creamer and sugar to her coffee. Then she stood sipping the brew, waiting for Brady to return.

The lieutenant showed up with a pretty woman with gray hair beside him. "Ms. Ramsey? This is Bethany."

"Hi." She set down her cup to shake the woman's hand. "Thanks for coming in early."

"I don't mind. I am so sorry you're going through this." It seemed Lieutenant Yale had filled Bethany in on her missing son. "Shall we get started?"

"Yes." She took her seat and sipped her coffee, watching

as Bethany set out her colored pencils and then put her sketchbook on an easel. Grace's fingers trembled as the importance of this sketch sank deep.

If she failed to create a good likeness of the guy in the hoodie, they'd never find the man who took Caleb. And that was unacceptable.

She took a deep breath and silently prayed. *Lord, give me the strength and wisdom to get this right!*

BRADY'S PHONE rang as he was getting the phone cable cord from the car. He frowned when he saw Rhy's number. "Hey, what's up?"

"I was hoping you'd tell me," Rhy responded dryly. "I saw the Amber Alert go out, and the kid in the photograph looks amazingly like you at that age."

Brady closed his eyes for a moment, realizing he should have warned his siblings. Their family photos were spread all over the house, including some of him as a young kid roughly Caleb's age. "Yeah, sorry about the shock. I just found out about him myself," he finally admitted.

"Wait, he's really your son?" Rhy's voice rose in surprise. "I mean, sure the kid looks just like you, but I was kidding."

"You remember my college girlfriend, Grace Ramsey? We were both at UW–Madison together?"

"She broke up with you shortly after you left for Virginia, right?"

"Two weeks after, yeah." He leaned against the side of the SUV. "She called last night to let me know Caleb had been kidnapped and that he was my son."

"Wow, Brady, that must have been tough." Rhy's voice

was full of sympathy. "But you should have called earlier. You know we're all ready and willing to help find him."

"I do know that." His family was phenomenal when it came to supporting each other. He had done the same for them too. "Unfortunately, we don't have much to go on. I have Matt Callahan and his K-9 Duchess searching Caleb's scent from his favorite stuffed animal we found in the parking lot of a local motel, but we haven't been able to narrow down where this guy is holding him."

Rhy let out a low whistle. "Do you know why Grace kept him a secret all these years?"

"She claims she broke things off because of her brother's illegal activity. He's in jail for investment fraud, and it's likely one of his victims is the one who set up the kidnapping."

"Yeah, right." Rhy didn't sound convinced.

"It's flimsy," Brady agreed. "And I own a piece of responsibility myself for not going to see her when I was finished with my training at Quantico. But that's in the past. Right now, all that matters is getting him back."

"That's true. We're here, Brady. Whatever you need, we'll get it for you."

"I may need cash for the ransom. Obviously, we'd do everything possible to make sure this guy doesn't escape with the money, but I will need enough to convince him to make the exchange."

"Done." Rhy didn't hesitate. "We'll scrape together whatever you need. Don't worry about that part of the equation. I'll rally the family as soon as the banks open. We can take out a home equity loan on the homestead, among finding other cash reserves. We can borrow against our pensions too. Whatever it takes. Just find your son."

His eyes burned with tears a mixture of gratitude and

love for his family, but he ruthlessly brushed them away. This wasn't the time to dwell on the years with Caleb that he'd lost. Not when his future with his son hung in limbo. "Oh, and keep this out of the news, will you? I haven't told my boss about the blood connection."

"I understand, you're worried he'll pull you from the case," Rhy agreed.

"Yes." Brady pushed away from the SUV. "I'll keep you posted on how things go."

"You better." Rhy paused, then added, "And congrats, Brady. I think you're the first Finnegan to start the next generation of Finnegans. Mom and Dad would be ecstatic if they were still with us."

"Yeah, they would." His throat tightened with emotion. "Later."

He felt oddly lighter as he headed back into the precinct. Knowing he always had family willing to cover his back was the best feeling on earth. The thought of Grace's only brother being in prison for fraud made him realize she didn't have that same level of camaraderie. Not that he and his brothers and sisters hadn't fought and argued, because they had. A lot. But in the end, every single one of them would do anything for the others.

Maybe he had a little sympathy for what Grace must have suffered over the past few years, but that wasn't a good excuse to keep Caleb a secret from him.

Inside the precinct, he watched Grace interacting with the sketch artist, a woman who appeared to be in her midfifties. He wanted to know how the sketch was coming along but forced himself to stay back. Hovering over Grace's shoulder would only add additional pressure and stress she didn't need.

Grace was as beautiful as he remembered. Even with

her green eyes weary with exhaustion, deep lines bracketing the corners of her mouth, and her porcelain skin overly pale. He'd loved her seven years ago and had been shocked when she'd broken things off, claiming she'd found someone else.

Yet he'd also let her go without even attempting to find out more about what had changed. Maybe it was his youthful arrogance, feeling as if she was the one who'd lost out on their relationship. He'd figured he was a good catch, and she was the one who'd be sorry to let him go.

His arrogance had been his downfall. Along with his pride. They'd both prevented him from going to see her. Yet he was the one who'd lost the most.

He'd lost his son.

He quietly plugged in Grace's phone, then went over to speak to Yale. "I have the motel clerk coming in with an officer from the scene. He should be here any minute. Anything more come through on the tip line?"

"Nothing useful yet, although there was this one guy." Yale rummaged on his desk. "Oh, here it is. A guy who works at a gas station claims a man came in to pay for gas with cash, and he also bought a lot of candy." Yale glanced up at him. "He didn't see a kid, but the amount of candy seemed odd, so he decided to call."

"Is his name Trent? Can I have his contact information?" Brady felt a surge of excitement. "He might be at the gas station near the motel where we know Caleb was held for a short while."

"Yeah, Trent Anderson." Yale arched a brow. "How did you know?"

"We spoke to the gas station owner early this morning." He pulled out his phone and dialed Trent's number. Unfortunately, the witness didn't answer, so he left a message identifying himself as an FBI agent working the case and requesting a call back. "It's interesting our UNSUB went there before he kidnapped the boy. I'm sure he bought the candy to use as a bribe."

"That's good news, but not sure it helps you now," Yale conceded.

"No, but between Grace, the motel clerk, and Trent, we should have a solid description of the guy to go on. As soon as those sketches are done, we'll plaster them all over the news with the Amber Alert."

"That should shake loose a few more sightings from the general public." Yale sighed. "Looks like our tip line will be busy."

"I have more agents and assistants coming to help manage the influx." He glanced at his watch. "They should be here by eight."

"Okay, that will help." Yale eyed him critically. "This case seems very personal to you."

"Any missing child is personal," he quickly shot back. Maybe too quickly because Yale's eyebrow only arched higher. He forced a smile and waved a casual hand. "Grace is an old friend."

"Uh-huh." Yale didn't look convinced but let the matter drop.

Tucking the note with Trent's information into his pocket, Brady turned to head back over to Grace and Bethany. His nerves were on edge; waiting patiently for Bethany to finish the sketch was not easy. And his stomach knotted when he overheard Grace fretting.

"I don't know why the nose doesn't seem right. Maybe try making it a little wider?" Her brow was furrowed with concentration.

"The motel clerk will be here soon," he said. "Don't

worry if you can't remember everything. He should be able to help fill in the blanks."

"You're assuming the kidnapper and the hoodie guy are one and the same," Grace said. "What if they're partners? It could be there are two men holding Caleb."

She had a good point. His gut told him there was only one kidnapper, but he knew better than to make assumptions. Best to deal with facts. "Okay, you're right. But don't stress, just do your best."

"Finnegan?" Yates gestured for him to come over. "We have a lead. A woman at a fast-food restaurant claims she saw a man with a boy looking like Caleb in a car seat in the back seat. They went through the drive-through."

"Where? Did she get a license plate number?"

"No. But the restaurant is only five miles from here." Yates ripped off a slip of paper from his notepad. "Here you go."

"Thanks." He glanced back to where Grace was still working on the sketch. There wasn't time to waste, so he shot out of the precinct and jumped into his SUV. He peeled away from the curb and used his hands-free function to call Marc. "Hey, meet me at the Quick Bites Breakfast and Burgers. Female employee working the drive-through said a man and a boy came through just five minutes ago."

"On it," Callahan said.

Brady drove as fast as he dared without having the benefit of red lights and sirens. He pulled up to the restaurant, raking his gaze over the parking lot, but didn't see a four-door dark Honda or any other car with a male driver and a car seat in the back.

He hurried inside and flashed his badge. "FBI! Who saw the man and the boy?"

"I did." A round middle-aged woman hurried over. "I

called as soon as I realized the missing boy was in the car seat."

"What's your name, ma'am?"

"Hetty Dunn. I'm the morning manager."

"Thanks for calling, Hetty. Does this restaurant have cameras?" He felt the need to ask, although so far they hadn't been fortunate enough to get this guy on camera. "Can I see the video?"

"No cameras, sorry. But I have a phone." Hetty pulled a phone with a broken screen from her pocket. "I mean, I tried to take a picture. Not sure it's any good, though."

"Let's see." He waited impatiently for her to unlock the phone and pull up her photos.

She grimaced and turned the camera. "I kept the phone hidden from his view and only got a glimpse of the side of his face."

"Anything is helpful, thank you." He peered at the photo, silently agreeing it wasn't much. "Would you mind if I texted this picture to my phone?" Without waiting for her to answer, he brought up the text app and typed in his phone number. Seconds later, his phone dinged with the incoming photo. "Thank you."

"He bought two breakfast sandwiches and a chocolate shake for the boy," Hetty continued. "I heard the boy tell him he wasn't hungry and wanted to go home, but the driver ignored him."

Brady tried to take comfort in the fact that the kidnapper was feeding Caleb. "Are you sure there was only one man in the car?"

"Yes, I'm positive." Hetty glanced over when Marc Callahan entered the restaurant holding up his badge. "I wish I could tell you more."

"You're doing fine." Brady did his best to sound reassuring, although a license plate would have been extremely helpful. "Can you tell us which direction he went when he left the restaurant?"

"I, uh"—she frowned, thinking hard—"yes, I'm pretty sure he turned right. I'm not sure which direction that is, maybe north?"

"No, ma'am, that's south," Marc corrected. "You're sure you didn't catch a license plate number? Or the make and model of the car?"

"Well, it was a black Honda, I know that much," Hetty said with a nod. "Just like on the Amber Alert."

Brady exchanged a long look with Marc. Was she really remembering the car from seeing it? Or just regurgitating what had come across the Amber Alert? This was a common phenomenon with some witnesses. In trying to be helpful, their enthusiasm could be tainted by what they thought the authorities wanted to hear, rather than giving them details strictly from their memory.

"Do you mind if I ask why you assumed the child in the car seat was Caleb?" Marc asked.

"Well, he was wearing the blue Avengers pajamas, but it was the way he said he wasn't hungry and wanted to go home that caught my attention." Hetty planted her hands on her broad hips. "It's highly unusual for a kid to turn down a chocolate shake. And the driver avoided looking at me too. That's why the picture isn't so good." Her expression fell. "I feel terrible that I didn't get the license plate number. That poor little boy."

"Did he pay with cash?" Brady asked.

"Yes, most people do." Hetty frowned. "Now that I think about it, he told me to keep the change."

"I'll call this in as the last-known location." Marc

reached for his phone. "We'll keep the BOLO out for the black four-door Honda."

Brady nodded, but inside he wanted to scream with frustration. Caleb had been here just ten minutes ago.

Ten minutes!

Yet they were still no closer to finding him.

CHAPTER FIVE

"Don't ever do that again!" The mean man's voice was so loud Caleb covered his ears. "You don't talk when we're by other people, understand?"

He wanted to go home but didn't say anything, afraid the mean man was going to hit him. His mother had swatted his butt once when he turned the dials on the stove. But it hadn't hurt. Not really. Caleb didn't trust this man not to hurt him.

"Here. Eat this and drink your shake." The man thrust the food at him. They were still in the car, but the man had parked the car someplace where there was lots of green grass and picnic tables. It looked nice, but the man wouldn't let him get out of the car. Caleb had no idea where they were going, but he was hungry, so he ate the breakfast sandwich. The chocolate shake was watery, but he sucked it down anyway.

"Maybe I should just drug you," the man muttered. "Then I wouldn't have to worry about you blabbing to everyone we see."

Caleb wasn't sure what drugging him meant, but he was afraid to find out. "I'll be good," he whimpered.

The man turned to glare at him. "You'd better. Or else!"

He sucked the straw, shrinking from the mean man. He wanted his mommy, and he wanted to go home. As he looked through the window, he also wanted to play in the park. Maybe if he didn't do anything to make the mean man mad, he'd let Caleb run around outside.

Maybe . . .

GRACE WAS KEENLY aware of Brady's absence. She told herself she was being ridiculous, but she couldn't sit still. Couldn't concentrate. It felt like her nerves were standing on edge.

The desk clerk from the motel, Andy Walsh, was doing a better job with the sketch than she had. And as he worked with Bethany, she realized the hoodie guy was the same man he'd seen at the motel.

Maybe there weren't two kidnappers. Unless one had stayed hidden as Brady suggested.

"That's him," she whispered when Bethany turned the sketch to Andy.

"Yep, that's the guy who was in room six," Andy agreed.

"You both did great," Bethany said with a reassuring smile. Grace knew Andy was the real hero in this. She hadn't been able to get the face right, but Andy nailed it. "I'll get this to Lieutenant Yale."

"Thank you, Andy." Grace tried to summon a smile, but her face felt like it might crack. "You were very helpful."

"Sure." Andy frowned. "If I'd known he had the kid . . ."

"It's okay. It's not your fault." Grace stood and

unplugged her phone from the charging cord. She had to find Brady. "Thanks again."

"Sure." Andy headed out of the precinct.

She called his number, hoping he wasn't just standing outside. It took several rings for him to answer.

"Hi, Grace. How is the sketch?"

"Where are you?" The question sounded so much like an accusation she winced. "I—uh the sketch is good thanks to Andy the motel clerk. Bethany gave it to Lieutenant Yale."

"That's great news. I'm on my way back to the precinct," Brady said. "I'll fill you in when I get there."

"Fill me in on what?" she asked, but Brady had already disconnected. Her pulse leaped with anticipation, although surely if Brady had found Caleb, he'd have told her.

Wouldn't he?

She turned and disconnected the charging cord, rolling it into a ball and placing it in her pocket. Officers were arriving at the precinct, eyeing her curiously as they huddled around various cubicles drinking coffee. A wave of annoyance hit hard; they should be out on the streets in their patrol cars, searching for her son!

"Ms. Ramsey?" Lieutenant Yale's voice drew her attention. "I'm leaving soon, but I wanted to introduce you to Lieutenant Krull. She's the day shift lieutenant in charge. I filled her in on the situation with your son."

"He's been missing for almost eight hours." Grace held the woman's gaze with defiance. "I need everyone here to get out to look for him."

"They will hit the road soon, right after roll call." Lieutenant Krull's eyes were sympathetic. "The additional sketch of the perp should help us find him."

Grace prayed she was right. She raked her hand

through her dark hair, feeling frustrated beyond belief. The time was seven forty in the morning, and the longer Caleb was out there with the hoodie guy, the harder it would be to find them.

For all they knew, hoodie guy had taken him down over the state line to Chicago. A city five times as big as Milwaukee.

"Grace?" Brady's voice was a welcome relief. She spun and ran toward him, even though a tiny part of her wanted to fall apart when she saw he was alone.

"Did you find something?" She grasped his arm.

"The manager of the Quick Bites restaurant called in a sighting of Caleb in a black four-door Honda sedan." He pulled her into his arms. "They were gone by the time we got there, but she managed to take a picture."

"Of Caleb?" Her heart raced.

"No, of the driver." Keeping one arm around her waist, Brady took out his phone and thumbed to the picture. "It's a little blurry and only his profile."

"That looks like him." She wished desperately that the woman had taken a picture of Caleb too. "What did she say? How did she know the boy was Caleb?"

"He was in a child booster seat in the back and complained that he didn't want a chocolate shake. He wanted to go home." Brady shrugged. "She thought his comments were odd, especially since most kids would jump all over the chance to have a chocolate shake."

The news was only slightly reassuring. "How did Caleb look? Was he hurt in any way?"

"She didn't see any bruises and noticed the man bought food for him, a sandwich not just the shake. That makes me think he's taking care of Caleb."

"Bringing him home to me would be taking care of

him." She strove for patience. "But I guess it's a relief to know he gave him something to eat."

Brady hugged her close and surprised her by kissing the top of her head. For a nanosecond, she remembered how well they'd fit together seven years ago, but then she shook off the memories. They weren't the same people they were back then. Too much had changed.

Besides, the only thing that mattered was finding Caleb.

"This is good news, Grace." He stroked his hand down her back before easing away to look down at her. "I was hoping to get a license plate number, but the witness did confirm the vehicle our other witness saw, which is important. And the fact that she noticed him in the first place means the public has taken the Amber Alert seriously. Now that it's daytime, more calls will likely come in."

She thought of all the officers who were already making their way out of the general area. Probably going over to wherever they held roll call. "Will there be enough people to answer the phones?"

"Yes. And additional FBI resources will be here soon too." He smiled. "We're ready to jump on any tips we receive. Oh, here's the sketch you guys did." His phone pinged with what she assumed was the updated Amber Alert. He let out a low whistle. "This is good, Grace. Really good. This should help us find him."

She prayed that was true. She couldn't wait for this nightmare to be over. To have Caleb back safe and sound. "When do you think the kidnapper will make the ransom call?"

"I'm sure he will do that very soon." Brady looked thoughtful. "It's possible he's driving around, waiting for the banks to open. I have a feeling the Amber Alert has him afraid to stay in one place too long."

"I hope you're right." The thought of receiving a ransom demand filled her with relief intermixed with dread. Despite the way things worked on TV, she knew there was a very real possibility the kidnapper would kill Caleb and take off with the cash.

Yet she trusted Brady and Marc Callahan enough to know they would do everything possible to make sure that didn't happen.

Please, Lord Jesus, keep Caleb safe in Your care!

"LET'S head to the FBI office." Brady cupped Grace's elbow in his palm to lead her outside. "We'll want to be somewhere quiet when the call comes in."

"Okay." Grace seemed subdued.

"We'll grab breakfast on the way." He glanced at her. "Don't argue, Grace. You need your strength. And we know Caleb has been given something to eat."

"Knowing that the kidnapper bought him food makes me feel slightly better." She climbed into the passenger seat of his SUV.

"I feel the same way." He'd almost purchased breakfast at the Quick Bites but wasn't sure what Grace would want to eat. Especially being under stress. "You want to use the Quick Bites drive-through? The same place the kidnapper took Caleb?"

"Yes, please." She shook her head with a wry smile. "It doesn't make sense that I would find comfort in eating food from there, but it does."

Emotions were rarely logical, but he was very glad Grace seemed in better spirits. Hopefully once she had something to eat, she'd feel even better.

He wasn't kidding about her needing strength to get through the next few hours. Once the ransom call came in, they would be working nonstop to set up a trap at the site of the exchange.

"You mentioned the banks opening at nine," Grace said. "Does that mean the FBI will begin pulling funds together then?"

He hesitated, then decided this wasn't the time to lie to her. "The FBI doesn't pay ransoms, Grace. But I have my family working on getting the funds together. We'll be able to get enough cash to convince the kidnapper he has whatever he's asked for."

"What?" Her hand shot out to grasp his arm. Her fingers dug painfully into him, but he didn't protest. "I thought the FBI would help us?"

"Grace, please trust me. We're going to be fine. My brother Rhy is already spreading the word throughout the family. I have no doubt we'll get the money we need."

"But what if he asks for some outrageous amount? Like tens of millions? We'll never pull together enough for that!" Her voice sounded panicked.

"My brother-in-law Bax Scala is loaded, and I suspect Kyleigh will ask him for help." He glanced over at her. "Especially since they know Caleb is my son too."

Sucking in a harsh breath, she abruptly let him go. "You told them?"

"Yes." He frowned. "Did you think I was going to keep this news a secret from my family? No way, Grace. Besides, Rhy guessed at the blood connection upon seeing Caleb's picture. They deserve to know, just as I did."

She glanced away, a flush creeping over her cheeks. "I know. I just . . . hoped for more time. They'll hate me."

"They won't. They may not like what you did, but they

would never hate you, Grace. That's not how Christians are taught."

"I hate the kidnapper." Her voice was so soft he had trouble hearing her. "I hate him more than anything in the world."

"That's different." Was it really? He honestly wasn't sure. Yet he couldn't deny the need to make her feel better. "He's breaking the law, holding an innocent boy against his will. That's not the same as making a poor decision."

"I made the right decision at the time."

"No, you didn't." He drew in a deep breath. "I'm sorry. Let's not fight about this, okay? We need to find our son."

She nodded, remaining silent as he pulled into the drive-through lane of the Quick Bites restaurant. The place was busier now, and it occurred to him that Hetty, the manager, may not have noticed Caleb if the kidnapper hadn't arrived so early.

He silently thanked God for her keen instincts zeroing in on the strained relationship between the driver and his son. And for picking up on Caleb's wish to go home.

He pulled over to the side of the restaurant and threw the gearshift into park. "We'll eat here."

"Okay." He was glad she didn't argue.

"Lord, we thank You for this food and ask that You please continue to keep our son, Caleb, safe in Your loving arms. Amen."

"Amen," Grace echoed.

They sat and ate in silence for several moments. Once they were finished, he put the gearshift into drive and left the parking lot. Ironically, he turned right, just like the kidnapper did, because it was the way to the office. Grace continued looking out the windows, no doubt searching for the black four-door Honda sedan. He kept an eye out for the car, too, but had a feeling the kidnapper had found a place to hide for a while.

At least, that's what Brady thought would be the most logical thing to do. Could be he was giving the kidnapper too much credit.

In his humble opinion, this particular UNSUB didn't seem very organized. Oh, he'd started out somewhat prepared, buying candy, getting gas, and making sure to have a car seat for Caleb before grabbing him from the bedroom. But since leaving the motel where Caleb had dropped Lucy, his stuffed dog, it appeared the guy had stayed on the road, maybe driving around while wondering what to do next. It could be why he'd gone through the Quick Bites drive-through, only to be identified by Hetty.

Two big breaks in the case so far, the drive-through restaurant and the motel where Caleb had dropped Lucy. Too bad the perp's fingerprints hadn't popped in the system. Although it made sense. This guy wasn't a professional criminal. He was just some guy trying to get his retirement investments back.

Or maybe his parents' investments?

He quickly called Marc. "Hey, do you have that list of the people who lost money from Adam Ramsey's investment scam? We need to start combing through that list to find anyone who looks like the sketch Grace and Andy did for us. The guy looks young, so maybe it's his parents who lost all their savings, and this guy is taking matters into his own hands to get the money back."

"I have one of our associates going through the list now," Marc confirmed. "I can add that piece, it's a good idea. No news yet on the ransom?"

"No, but I have a sense he'll call very soon." He eyed the clock. It was going on eight thirty.

"Matt and Duchess have come up empty-handed. He's taking her home to feed her breakfast and to get some rest," Marc said. "I told him that was a good idea; we want Duchess fresh in case we get a tip on the boy's location."

"I agree." He glanced at Grace, who looked depressed at the news. "I'm thinking the motels are a dead end anyway. The minute this guy realizes we have his likeness plastered all over the television, he'll avoid public places."

"That was my thought too." Marc paused, then asked, "Are you and Grace heading to the office?"

"Yes, we're almost there. I figure it might be nice to be at the office if she gets the call."

"Ping me the moment you get a demand," Marc said. "I've been keeping tabs on the other aspects of the investigation. The DNA is being processed, but since this guy's fingerprints aren't in the system, I doubt the DNA will be a match either."

"I think the list of investors is our best bet in finding this guy." Brady saw the FBI office building up ahead. "I'll continue working on that with the rest of the team."

"Sounds good. Keep in touch." Marc disconnected from the call.

"You really think the hoodie guy is the son of someone who lost money to my brother?" Grace asked.

"I think it's very likely," he agreed. "Which is good for us. It's better he's not a professional kidnapper, and that he cares about his parents. I think that explains why he stopped to get food for Caleb. If this guy only wants money, I doubt he'll hurt our son."

"I pray you're right about that," Grace whispered. "It's hard enough knowing Caleb is with a stranger, but to be hurt by this man would be so much worse."

"I agree." He pulled into the parking lot of the office

building. "Does Caleb go to church? Have you taught him to believe in God?"

"No." She didn't meet his gaze. "I fell away from the church after discovering my brother's fraudulent activities. My brother hurt so many people . . ." Her voice trailed off.

"His sins are not yours, Grace." He was disappointed his son couldn't lean on God and prayer during this difficult time. "And Caleb would benefit from knowing our Lord Jesus."

She didn't say anything in response to that, so he let it drop. To be fair, it was a moot point now. But when they had Caleb back safe and sound, he would make sure Caleb learned about God and faith.

It was one of many things he wanted his son to know about. It wasn't the time to discuss details of their future as co-parents to Caleb now, but if Brady had his way, the first thing he'd do would be change Caleb's last name to Finnegan.

He pushed out of the SUV and went around to help Grace. The meal had given her some energy, so she didn't lean on him as heavily as she had back at the precinct.

But he intended to be there for her no matter what. Not just because she was the mother of their son.

Seeing her again after all these years made him realize he still had feelings for her. He'd hoped to one day marry her, but obviously that hadn't happened. Yet despite the way she'd lied to him, and worse kept Caleb from him, he cared about her.

More than he should.

No point in letting Grace break his heart a second time. Especially not now. His parents had been wonderful role models, and his older siblings had also managed to find similar soul mates. Watching the love that radiated between

Rhy and Devon, Tarin and Joy, and Kyleigh and Bax, he would not settle for anything less.

And it was painfully obvious that Grace had not loved him the way he'd loved her.

He led the way inside, nodding at other agents who, he belatedly realized, looked at him strangely as he wasn't wearing his usual suit and tie. He'd completely forgotten to run home and change. Not that it mattered.

"Finnegan." Donovan Grady, the Special Agent in Charge of the entire Milwaukee office, was waiting for him when they entered. Donovan was at least fifteen years older than his thirty-three and rarely smiled. Today was no exception. "I need a word."

"Yes, sir." He glanced at Grace. "If I could get Ms. Ramsey set up in an interview room first, though, that would be helpful. We expect the kidnapper to make contact to demand a ransom very soon. I want to make sure the tech team is ready to trace the call."

If anything, Donovan's scowl deepened. "Five minutes."

He nodded and turned to head through a set of double glass doors. He flagged a fellow agent as he went. "Jim, I need you to make sure the tap is set up for Ms. Ramsey's phone. Can you do that?"

"It is all set. This way." His colleague gestured to the interview room where a tech was sitting in front of a computer. "Ian has it ready to go."

"Great, thanks." He pushed into the conference room and introduced Grace to Ian. "I need to talk to the SAC. I'll be back shortly."

"Okay." Ian appeared calm and relaxed.

He didn't want to leave Grace alone but decided it was best to get this confrontation with Donovan over with as soon as possible. He did not want to miss the ransom call.

He went into the office but remained standing. "Sir?"

"Why did this victim, Grace Ramsey, call you directly in the middle of the night?" Donovan's blunt question caught him off guard, although he should have expected it.

"We knew each other in college, sir. She knew I was with the FBI and needed my help." He did his best to appear nonchalant. "It seemed the trail was hot, so I followed it, bringing Callahan in to assist."

Donovan drummed his fingers on the desk. "Are you sure there isn't anything more to this? I'm tempted to remove you from the case."

He prayed the flash of panic wasn't visible in his gaze. "I'm sure, sir. Callahan is doing most of the legwork. We have a sketch of the UNSUB and expect him to make contact very soon. I believe we'll wrap this up before the end of the day."

"Feeling overconfident, aren't you?" Donovan stared at him for a long moment. "Next time you might want to call me first, before reaching out to other agents. Callahan was working another case for me, which meant I had to juggle things around."

He stiffened. "A missing child trumps everything."

"Yes, and that's the only reason you're both still working the case." Donovan waved an impatient hand toward the door. "Go, but keep me in the loop from now on."

"Yes, sir. Oh, one more thing. Would you reach out to the Chicago FBI office? I would like an agent to speak personally with Adam Ramsey. It's possible he knows who this perp is, maybe even hired the guy to do the deed."

"Yes, I'll do that," Donovan grudgingly agreed.

"Thank you." He gave his boss a tight nod, then left. His gut churned with anger, but he did his best to push it aside.

Donovan was right about the fact that Brady should

have called him first. Frankly, it hadn't even occurred to him. He'd needed someone to help on the street, and that was not Donovan's role. Brady didn't care much for office politics. Most of the time, Donovan was a decent boss. Brady wasn't usually stuck in the hot seat. Well, it was too late to change anything now. He shrugged off the pointed conversation and entered the conference room.

"Anything?" he asked, his gaze darting between Grace and Ian.

"Not yet." Grace had her phone sitting on the table near the computer. "Ian says he might be able to trace a short call."

"Ian is one of the best." He dropped into the seat beside Grace. "Remember what I said about speaking to Caleb."

"Trust me, I won't forget." She looked stronger, as if she'd been refueled by the coffee and food. "It's getting close to nine o'clock, Brady. Why hasn't he called?"

"He will." Brady couldn't imagine the guy had done all of this for nothing. Yet this guy could also be a bit unhinged. Maybe even regretting his rash action of kidnapping a child.

The seconds ticked by slowly. When Grace's phone rang, they both jumped. Ian, however, still looked calm.

"Unknown number," Ian said, hitting several keys on his computer keyboard. "Go ahead and answer, Grace."

Grace hit the answer button, and the speaker button so that he could hear the conversation. "Hello? Who is this?"

"You want your kid? You can have him for five million dollars. I have an offshore account ready to accept the transfer."

"Yes, I want Caleb. I'll get the money transferred, but only after I know you haven't hurt him. I demand to talk to my son."

There was a brief pause, then the kidnapper said, "Talk to your mom but make it quick."

"Mommy?" Caleb's frightened voice ripped a hole in Brady's gut. "Will you please come and get me?"

"Sure, baby, I will. But I need you to tell me something. What's the name of your stuffed animal?"

"Lucy. I lost her, Mommy." Caleb's sobs came through the line. "I lost Lucy."

"It's okay. I love you, Caleb. Don't be afraid, I love you." Grace's eyes welled with tears.

"Enough." The kidnapper's voice came back on the line. "Five million ready to transfer by one in the afternoon. I'll call you back with more details as to how this exchange will take place."

And with that, the call ended as abruptly as it started.

CHAPTER SIX

"Caleb? Wait, don't hang up!" Grace gripped her phone so tightly she thought it might break. She finally set it down and swiped at her face. Hearing her son's voice, knowing he was scared to death, tore at her heart. She swallowed hard and looked at Ian. "Did you get a location? Can you tell me where he's being held?"

"The phone pinged off a cell tower located in Oakdale, which isn't that far from here." Ian grimaced. "Although that tower covers a twenty-mile radius."

Twenty miles? Her heart sank. "There has to be a way to pinpoint his location."

"Let's get that five-million demand to the team going through Adam Ramsey's investors," Brady said. "Maybe that will help narrow down the suspect pool."

"But we have to find Caleb!" Grace protested.

"I know, that's our priority. I thought I heard birds chirping in the background," Brady said thoughtfully. "They could be outside, maybe at a park. He'd want to avoid other people, right?"

"That's a good point." Ian worked the keyboard. "Here

we go, Fall River Park is in the radius of that cell tower. The number was listed as unknown, but I will work with the cell companies to get more information." Ian grimaced. "It may take a little time, though."

Time they didn't have! Grace battered down a wave of frustration and jumped to her feet. "We have to go to the park, right now!"

"Hold on a minute." Brady had his phone to his ear. "Matt? Can you and Duchess get over to Fall River Park in Oakdale? We have reason to believe the kidnapper might still be there with Caleb. And do me a favor, make sure you go incognito. I know usually Duchess wears a K-9 vest to work, but I don't want to spook this guy into running, especially if he's hanging out there with Caleb." He listened for a moment, then added, "Thanks, I'm heading there too with Grace. Stay in touch, okay?"

Knowing Duchess would be on Caleb's scent helped her feel better. This could work. They might find him before the one o'clock deadline. "What about sending the Oakdale police to swarm the area?"

"I'll call a couple of cops to head over undercover in street clothes, but I don't want to flood the area with uniformed officers. That would spook him into running away. It's better if we can get eyes on our perp without his knowing we're there."

That made sense, and a blossom of hope bloomed in her heart. She followed Brady out of the FBI office building and back to his SUV. The sooner they got to Fall River Park, the better. She desperately wanted to find her son.

She listened as Brady asked for undercover Oakdale officers to head to Fall River Park. When he finished, he quickly pulled out of the parking lot. "Try not to get too excited," he warned as he drove. "This kidnapper might not be the smartest guy on the planet, but there is a good chance he left as soon as he made the call."

"I know." She understood his concern, but it was too late. Her hopes were sky high. "What about getting the cash together for the exchange?"

In response, he spoke out loud. "Call Rhy." A moment later, she heard his older brother's voice on the line.

"Hey, Brady. What's the latest?"

"Five-million ransom by one o'clock this afternoon. He wants a wire transfer, so we'll have to find a way to make it look like we can transfer that amount, even if we don't have it. Like I said earlier, I am hoping we can stop this guy before he can escape with the ransom demand."

"I'm on it," Rhy said. "Bax offered to fund the entire amount."

"I'm hoping we don't need the entire amount," Brady protested. "I would feel bad if this perp managed to get away with the money."

"Honestly, I don't think Bax cares if he loses the money or not. He's more worried about Caleb."

Grace didn't know who Bax was but figured he must be a close friend of the family. A very rich close friend of the family.

"We're heading to Fall River Park in Oakdale, the kidnapper's phone pinged off a cell tower there," Brady explained. "Ian our tech specialist is trying to find out the cell number and who the number belongs to. I'm sure it's a disposable phone, so that may take a while."

"That's a great lead. In the meantime, we'll work on the financial end of this. Bax said he'd free up the funds, putting them in a special account to be transferred if needed. You keep searching for this guy and your son. Keep me in the loop, okay?"

"Will do, thanks, Rhy."

"Who is Bax?" Grace asked when he ended the call.

"Assistant District Attorney Baxter Scala, he's Kyleigh's husband. They got married at the end of April. They were going to wait until May but moved it up as Elly is graduating from her EMT program this month."

"And he has five million dollars?"

"Apparently, he inherited money from his Italian grandparents and invested well." Brady shrugged. "He's probably the nicest rich guy I know."

She remembered thinking that once about her brother, Adam. Now, not so much. It made her so angry to know her son was in danger because of what her brother had done. Being sentenced to eighteen years in jail seemed too good for him.

What if something happened to Caleb? No, she couldn't go there. She'd just heard her son's voice. The kidnapper had bought him breakfast. He was scared, but he would survive.

Staying strong when your world crumbled to pieces wasn't easy. She found herself reaching out to take Brady's hand.

"I hope we find him," she whispered.

"We will." Brady spoke with confidence. Then he sweetly raised her hand to his mouth to kiss it. "And don't forget that we have dozens of people working this case. Something will break before the deadline."

"And if it doesn't?"

"You'll meet with the kidnapper, and we'll find a way to transfer the money in exchange for our son." Brady made it sound so simple when she knew it would be anything but. "Trust me, Grace. We'll make this work no matter what. I know it's not easy but put your faith in God and in the hardworking men and women in law enforcement."

"I do trust you, Brady. And I've been praying for God to keep Caleb safe." She put a hand to her stomach, hoping to settle her nerves. "It was so hard to hear him crying on the phone. I hate that man for what he's putting Caleb through."

"I feel the same way, but dwelling on that isn't going to help." Why did Brady always have to sound so reasonable? "We need to think positive. To believe that Caleb will get through this."

She swallowed the urge to snap at him because she knew he was right. Fluctuating emotions clouded reasonable judgment. "I was thinking we should look in the area around the park's restrooms. It seems to make sense that Caleb would need to go after eating."

"That's a very good idea." Brady's voice rang with admiration. Using his thumb, he made another call. "Matt? Start searching with Duchess at the restrooms."

"Already making our way there," Matt responded. "Having two kids of my own, I'm very familiar with little kids needing to use the bathroom."

"Great, thanks. We're nearing the park now. Let me know if Duchess picks up Caleb's scent."

"I will. Talk to you later." Matt didn't wait for a response before ending the call.

"This is going to work," Grace whispered. She stared down at her hand in Brady's. "It has to."

Brady didn't say anything as he drove. When he finally pulled into a small parking lot near the park entrance, he threw the gearshift into park, then turned in his seat to face her. "Dear Lord Jesus, we beg You to continue holding our son Caleb safe in Your loving arms. Amen."

"Amen." The tightness in her chest eased just a bit. "Thank you."

"Always," Brady said, gently squeezing her hand. Then he glanced around the area. "No black four-door Honda sedan here. That makes me wonder if there are other small parking lots scattered around the park. I haven't been here before, have you?"

"No. I don't have a car. The day care center has a van, but I generally don't use it for personal trips." She shrugged, feeling helpless. "Maybe we should drive around a bit. We know for sure the kidnapper has a car."

"Sounds good to me." He put the SUV in gear and backed out of the parking space. Soon they were driving through an area that had lots of trees on either side of the road.

Under different circumstances, the scenic drive would be pretty. Yet all she could think about was that if Caleb had managed to get free, he would end up getting lost in the woods. What if there was water nearby too? She shivered, praying there weren't other hazards that she wasn't aware of.

They didn't see any cars as they drove. Upon reaching a picnic area, two cars came into view. One was a white SUV, the other a blue truck.

"He might have taken Caleb away by now." She twisted her fingers as Brady continued driving. "This could be nothing but a waste of time."

"Following up leads on an investigation is never a waste of time," Brady said firmly. "You can't think about it that way. We're making sure the kidnapper isn't still here. And that's important."

"I know, I'm sorry." She struggled to rein in her

emotions. "You're right. The park is bigger than I expected. We still may find him."

"That's the spirit." Brady straightened in his seat. "I think those are the restrooms up ahead."

She craned her neck and caught a glimpse of dark wood through the budding trees. The road widened, and Brady pulled over to park next to the other SUV that was already there. She recognized it as Matt Callahan's by the K-9 emblem on the side and the crated area in the back for Duchess.

"Let's get out and see if Duchess has found anything." Brady hadn't even brought the SUV to a stop when she was out of the car and hurrying toward the brown building.

"Grace, wait. Don't interfere with Duchess," Brady called.

She stopped, seeing Matt and Duchess up ahead. The dog was doing her zigzag thing again, her nose going from the ground to the air as she followed some invisible scent trail only she could recognize.

Grace held her breath as the beautiful black-and-brown German shepherd abruptly stopped and sat near the side of the building.

"Good girl, Duch," Matt praised, tossing a toy into the air for her to catch. "Good girl."

Without hesitation, Grace ran over to where the K-9 had alerted on Caleb's scent. It was the men's room, but she didn't care. Heading inside, she looked in the two stalls, then turned away when she realized they were empty.

Caleb wasn't here now, but he had been. And recently. She wanted to rant and rave and scream at the top of her lungs.

But she didn't. Instead, she prayed that Duchess might

be able to keep tracking Caleb, leading them to where he was being held right now.

"HAS DUCHESS ALERTED ANYWHERE ELSE?" Brady asked Matt.

"Near the edge of the parking lot. Here, I'll show you." Matt turned and led the way to a spot he'd marked with a small rock. "I figure the perp parked here and took the kid inside the bathroom, then brought him straight back to the car."

It was what he'd feared, but it had been worth a try. "Okay, can you still search the area around here? Just to be sure?"

"Of course." Matt's blue eyes were full of empathy. "The good news is that Duch likes this game of seek."

The dog's tail wagged vigorously as if in agreement.

"We're going to keep driving through the park, looking for the black Honda sedan." Brady gestured to the wooded area around the restrooms. "If you find anything else, call me. Otherwise, when we're finished here, we'll head back to the FBI office."

"Understood." Matt bent to scratch Duchess behind the ears. "She was a little confused at first when I asked her to track Caleb without her vest being on. That's usually her signal to work. Thankfully, she found his scent anyway."

"She's amazing," Brady agreed. "Too bad this guy is taking Caleb around in his car. If they were on foot, Duchess would find him in a heartbeat."

"That does put a wrench in her ability to track him." Matt shrugged. "But we're here if you get another lead. I worked with my boss, and he agreed to free us up for the rest of the day to work this case."

"Thanks, Matt." Brady was touched by his cousin's willingness to jump in to help. Then again, Matt was the father of two small kids. There was nothing worse than knowing your child was in danger.

Especially a child you'd never been able to hug and kiss good night. To read bedtime stories to or play ball with in the backyard.

A wave of grief over what he'd missed hit hard. Brady thrust it aside with an effort. Going back was not an option. He knew that all he could do was look forward. Besides, it was time to take his own advice and think positive. They'd narrowed down the location where their UNSUB had made his ransom call. Duchess confirmed Caleb had been here and maybe wasn't too far away.

Unless, of course, the kidnapper drove to the other side of the city. Brady didn't really think he would, though. For one thing, the guy wouldn't want to waste gas. Not with the Amber Alert out there. No, he felt certain the guy had chosen this park in the first place to stay out of the public eye.

"Hey, Matt, maybe we should check the other parks in the area." He pulled out his phone to do a quick search. "This guy may be trying to stay away from restaurants and other places with lots of customers. I'm sure he'd search for another place just like this."

"Okay, what do you have in mind?" Matt came over to peer over his shoulder. Grace crowded close too.

"That park has several large playgrounds, including a skateboard rink," she said, pointing at the next closest park.

"Too crowded, he wouldn't want to risk being seen by other parents of children. Every mother in the area has probably seen the Amber Alert." He scrolled through the other possibilities. "There's a park closer to the lakefront, but that doesn't seem to have many hiding places either."

"What about another nature-like park outside of Oakdale?" Matt suggested. "I know there's one in Greenland."

"Yeah." He worked his phone. "There are two other nature parks that aren't too far away. We'll take White Park while you head to Greenland Park."

"Got it." Matt turned away. "Come, Duchess."

"You really think he'll stick to parks?" Grace asked as they headed for his SUV.

"I do." He had nothing but his gut instincts to go on, and he prayed they wouldn't fail him now. "Why wouldn't he? As you said, they all have restrooms available. It's also a good way to stay off the radar."

"Okay, let's go." Grace slid into the passenger seat.

"We're going to drive through the rest of Fall River Park first." He glanced at her as he backed up. "Keep your eyes peeled for a black or dark Honda."

"What if he's changed cars?" Grace gnawed her lower lip. "I'm worried that we may be giving too much credit to my neighbor's glimpse of the kidnapper's car as it disappeared from sight."

"The restaurant witness said it was a four-door black Honda too." He shrugged, remembering his concern that Hetty had only repeated what she'd heard on the Amber Alert. "Don't worry, the investigation doesn't just hinge on the car. We have the sketch you and Andy worked on together, and the team going through the investors who may have lost five million from your brother's scam."

"Yes, I know, but why haven't we heard anything about that yet?" She didn't sound accusatory, just upset. The stress was taking a toll on her. "I mean, how many large investors could my brother have stolen money from?"

"I'm not sure, but I trust they'll call me if they find something." Thinking of the FBI office made him remember his promise to Donovan. He quickly placed the call, inwardly relieved when his boss didn't pick up. "This is Finnegan, we followed a lead from where the kidnapper's cell phone pinged off a cell tower not far from a park. A local cop and his K-9 found the boy's scent at Fall River Park near the restrooms. We're heading over to check the other parks nearby. Call me if you have questions." He ended the call, glancing at Grace. "My boss expects regular updates."

"Is this how kidnappings usually go?" She sounded so dejected he wished he could take her into his arms and hold her close. "You find a promising lead, then nothing?"

He didn't want to tell her that he'd seen kidnappings go wrong. Not often, but one dead child was more than enough. There had been a custody kidnapping a few years back where the perp had killed the child, then himself. It had been awful. He spoke with confidence he didn't quite feel. "Every scenario is different. I told you before, this guy comes across as an amateur. There's no way to know exactly what he'll do next, but the fact that he made a ransom demand is a good sign. That tells me that he's in this for the money, nothing more. Caleb sounded scared, but he didn't mention being hurt. I don't think this guy wants to harm him."

"I pray you're right," Grace murmured.

He did too. Hearing his son's cries had been difficult, but the little boy had answered Grace's question about his stuffed dog. The break in the case hadn't gotten the results he'd wanted. Oh, he was thankful Duchess had found

Caleb's scent, but heading to the parks to keep searching seemed like a shot in the dark.

Yet he couldn't force himself to turn around and head back to the office without first checking them out.

They arrived at White Park fifteen minutes later. According to the map, it was bigger than Fall River Park, which was not great news. He tried to stay positive as he entered the park. "Watch for restroom signs, you know Caleb better than I do, but it's probably safe to assume he may have asked the kidnapper for another bathroom break."

"Good idea." She sighed and rubbed her temple. "I may need a break myself."

"Me too." He scanned the few cars parked along the side of the road but didn't see any dark four-door sedans. Which was a little strange as that was a popular model and color.

"Brady? I saw a restroom sign pointing straight ahead."

"Thanks." He'd been so focused on the cars he'd missed it. After rounding the curve, he saw the stone and wood structure. There were a couple of cars parked in front of the restrooms.

One of them was a black sedan. It was a Chevy, not a Honda, but his heart thumped with anticipation.

"A black car!" Grace practically shouted.

"I see it." He kept going for another few yards before pulling off the side of the road. "You stay here. I'll check it out."

"Caleb doesn't know you," she protested.

"It's a Chevy not a Honda, so it's probably not our kidnapper. Just give me a few minutes to check things out." He shoved his door open and jumped out. He didn't stay on the road but cut through the woods so that he could approach the building from behind.

Even though he knew this was probably nothing, antici-pation hummed through his veins. Keeping his hand on the butt of his gun, he darted through the trees, going from cover to cover in a zigzag pattern that reminded him of Duchess.

Soon he was creeping along the back of the building. There were sounds coming from the women's bathroom, so he crept up to the men's room.

But didn't hear anyone inside. Without waiting another moment, he ducked inside and swept his gaze around.

Empty.

He left the men's room in time to see the black Chevy backing out of the parking space. Reacting instinctively, he drew his weapon and raced forward. "FBI! Stop!"

The car jerked to a stop, and the woman behind the wheel lifted her hands up in surrender. He winced, feeling guilty for scaring her, but went over to check the back seat anyway.

A little boy was back there, but he looked younger than Caleb. It occurred to him that she may have taken him into the women's room with her.

He opened her driver's side door. "What's going on?" Her voice was lined with panic. "Who are you looking for?"

"I'm sorry to frighten you, but I'm following up on the Amber Alert issued earlier this morning." He holstered his weapon and offered a wan smile. "You didn't happen to see a man with a six-year-old boy, did you?"

"I don't think so." She slowly lowered her hands. Then understanding dawned. "Oh, it's my car, right? I heard on the news that the kidnapper was driving a black Honda."

"That's right." He took a step back. "Again, I'm sorry to frighten you."

"You know, I drove by a black Honda that was parked

along the side of the road on my way in," she said. "I remember thinking about the Amber Alert as I went past, but the vehicle appeared empty."

"Which way did you come in?" After the way he'd over-reacted to her vehicle, he told himself not to put too much credence into her comment.

"I, uh, from the west?" She wrinkled her brow, then glanced toward the east. In Milwaukee it was easy to keep track of directions when you had the sun rising over Lake Michigan each morning. Then she turned to look in the opposite direction. "Yes, from the west."

"Okay, thanks." He took another step back. "Again, I apologize for scaring you. Enjoy the rest of your day."

She rolled up her window and drove off. Brady jogged back to the car, somewhat surprised to see Grace was still sitting in the passenger seat, waiting for him.

"What happened?" she asked when he slid in behind the wheel.

"False alarm. But we'll keep driving. The woman back there saw a black four-door Honda sedan parked along the road."

"Here?" Grace grasped his arm. "Really?"

"She came into the park from the opposite direction that we did." He pulled out onto the road and gave the SUV more gas. If the vehicle was empty, the kidnapper may have taken Caleb to a secluded picnic table to sit and wait.

He tried to remain calm as he drove along the winding road, but when they made it through the entire park, reaching the entrance without seeing the black car, his spirits plummeted.

"Maybe it's on a different road," Grace said. "Please keep looking."

"Okay." He turned around and made the loop back

toward the restrooms. There was one road off to the left that he took, but there was no black four-door Honda in sight. Still, he circled the entire park again, just to be sure.

If the vehicle had been here, it was gone now.

"No, this can't be happening. You said she saw it!" Grace thumped her hand against the window. "We couldn't have missed him again."

He pulled over to the side of the road and turned to face her. "We'll keep searching until we find him."

Grace's green eyes filled with tears. Then she unbuckled her seatbelt and crawled over the center console and into his arms. He crushed her close, burying his face in her hair as she sobbed against him.

Wishing it hadn't taken a nightmare like this to bring them back together.

CHAPTER SEVEN

When her tears were spent, Grace rested against Brady, unwilling to move despite the uncomfortable position. To be this close to finding their son, only to lose him again, was heartbreaking.

Yet somehow, Brady's strong arms and his murmured reassurances helped beat back the panic that seized her. Grateful for his presence and his determination to get Caleb back, she realized just how unfair she'd been to keep Caleb a secret. Brady was an honorable man who'd deserved better.

The middle console was digging into her hip, so she reluctantly lifted her head and used the steering wheel to push off him. "Um, sorry about that."

"I'm not." His deep voice rumbled near her ear, sending shivers of awareness down her spine. The feelings she'd had for him came rushing back, reminding her of what she'd thrown away.

For his sake, at first.

She turned to apologize again, but he surprised her by angling his head and capturing her mouth with his. As if the embrace hadn't been wonderful enough, his kiss brought even more memories bubbling to the surface.

But then the kiss was over too soon as he gently helped her get back over the console and into her seat. "I'm sorry. I didn't mean to take advantage of the situation," he said. "Please forgive me."

"I'm the one who should apologize." She shook her head and met his gaze. "I never should have kept Caleb a secret from you."

"No, you should not have." He looked grimly disappointed for a moment, but then the darkness in his brown eyes vanished. "I can't lie and say I'm not upset about missing six years of my son's life, but there's nothing we can do to change that. It's done. As I said before, we need to stay focused on moving forward."

"I wouldn't blame you if you hated me," she whispered.

"I could never hate you, Grace." Brady started the car. "Never."

His words brought a warm glow to her heart, one she shouldn't even care about while her son was still in the hands of some creepy kidnapper. She gave herself a mental shake and tried to think about their next steps.

"We know Caleb was probably here," she said thoughtfully. "So maybe the kidnapper will show up at Greenland Park."

"We don't honestly know that Caleb was here for sure," Brady said. "All we know is that one woman saw a black Honda sedan, and she thought it was empty, but maybe it wasn't. It could be someone just pulled over to answer a text or something. With his or her head down, it may have looked empty at first glance."

"But you said the kidnapper might hang out at parks."

"It's a theory, yes. But one sighting of a car doesn't mean

much. That vehicle could have belonged to anyone. There are lots of Hondas on the road."

She didn't appreciate Brady being so casually logical about this. "Okay, but that doesn't mean Caleb isn't at another park. We need to keep searching for him."

"We will." He sighed. "I want to find him as much as you do."

"I know." She sat back against the seat, feeling abruptly exhausted. The highs and lows of this case were driving her insane. Yet no matter how tired she was, she would not rest until Caleb was safe.

Brady's phone rang, startling her. He used the buttons on his steering wheel to answer the call. "Finnegan."

"Got your message," a curt voice said. "The team has identified several possible suspects after combing through the victims of the investment scam. I've sent the list to your email."

"Thanks, Donovan," Brady replied. "Did they have anyone in particular that we can dig into first?"

"There are three that fit your top profile of a son seeking retribution for funds their parents had lost." There was a brief pause before Donovan added, "Lawrence Abrams, Joseph Custer, and Dominic Powers. We don't have dates of birth for them, so that will make it more difficult to find them."

Brady repeated the names, glancing at her curiously. "Thanks, boss. We're on our way back to the office. We'll need to go through their social media files to see if any of them look like our UNSUB."

"Fine, let me know if any of those pop for you," Donovan said. "Later."

Brady hit a button ending the call. "Do any of those names sound familiar to you?"

"No, but looking at their social media sites for photos is a great idea." A surge of excitement hit hard. "If we can identify the kidnapper, you'll be able to find his license plate number, right?"

"Yes." Brady hit the gas, quickly passing the slower traffic. She wished he could use red lights and sirens like the local police could. "I'm anxious to start looking through the list of suspects to compare them to your sketch."

"The motel clerk was the one who got most of the details, right? If we find someone that's close to a match, you may want to get Andy back to the office to identify him."

"If the sketch is a close match, that will be enough to get a search warrant to find this guy," Brady said grimly.

"That's good." She frowned. "I think he must be from out of town, likely the Chicago area. I know my brother had investors located all over, but his not being from Milwaukee would explain why he's hanging out at local parks."

"I thought of that too," Brady admitted. "But I didn't want to focus on out-of-state license plates, he could have easily rented a car near the airport. Especially if he took the train in from Chicago."

"Yeah, you're right." After all, she'd taken the train from Chicago to Milwaukee herself six years ago. After she'd given an anonymous tip to the Securities Exchange Commission about her brother's fraudulent practices. Yet even after she'd made that call, it had taken them more than four years to arrest Adam. Plus another nine months for the case to move through the system. It wasn't until her brother had been sent to a federal prison to serve his time that she'd rested easy.

Until now.

"I wonder why this guy waited so long to try to get his

money back." She grabbed the armrest when Brady made a fast turn. "Adam's been in prison for over a year now."

"Maybe it took him that long to find you. And to come up with a viable plan." Brady grimaced. "Although he still didn't plan it very well."

"He hasn't been caught yet," she pointed out.

"True. But we're getting close. I can feel it." Brady hit the gas again, passing several cars on the interstate, clearly in a hurry to get back to the FBI offices.

"I pray you're right." His enthusiasm was infectious.

Five minutes later, they reached the FBI office building. Brady escorted her inside, heading for a cubicle first to grab his laptop computer off his desk, before detouring to the conference room they'd used earlier.

Ian was still there. He glanced at them in surprise. "I don't have a name and number yet, I'm still working on it."

"We have some potential suspects too. I may need your help, though." Brady booted up his computer. "There are three names we need to dig into. Are you ready?"

"Yep." Ian gave a nod.

"Lawrence Abrams, Joseph Custer, and Dominic Powers," Brady said. "I'll take Lawrence. You take Joseph. We want to compare any recent photos of them to the sketch."

"Got it."

"What can I do?" Grace didn't like sitting there doing nothing.

"I'll need you in a few minutes." Brady did not look away from his computer screen. "Maybe more than a few," he added with a sigh. "It appears like there are more Lawrence or Larry Abramses than I anticipated."

"Same with the Joseph Custers," Ian added. "All three

of these guys could be going by shortened versions of their name. Dom, Nick, Joe, Joey, Larry, Law, et cetera."

The flicker of hope in her heart dimmed. Identifying their kidnapper suspect could take hours.

Hours they didn't have.

BRADY HAD to force himself to slow down, taking each matching name that popped up on the social media site one at a time, peering intently at each photograph. The last thing he needed was to rush and miss the suspect entirely.

Of course, some of these guys used their pets as a cover photo, which meant delving deeper into their site. Not always easy if they had privacy settings enabled.

"I'm going to get more coffee." Grace stood. "Would either of you like some?"

"I'm good," Ian said absently.

"That would be great." He tore his gaze from the computer to offer her a reassuring smile. Their brief but electric kiss flashed in his mind. "Thank you."

Grace nodded and slipped from the conference room. He watched her walk away for a moment, before dragging his attention back to the task at hand. It was tempting to narrow the search to Larry or Lawrence Abrams in the Chicago area, but he decided to use an age range instead.

That didn't help much. Swallowing a groan, he continued searching through the photos one by one.

Grace returned with his coffee, then asked, "Don't you have a third computer? I can go through social media sites too."

"I'll get her one," Ian said. "I need a break anyway."

"Okay, thanks." He took a sip of his coffee. He wanted

to warn her not to get her hopes up too high but held his tongue. She'd already experienced the turmoil of an investigation, so it wouldn't be her first disappointment.

Besides, he felt certain one of these three guys was their kidnapper. They just had to find him.

It didn't take long for Ian to return with another laptop for Grace. He signed in under his own name, then turned it to face her. "Don't forget to use all the various nicknames for Dominic," he told her.

"I won't." She eagerly went to work.

They sat in silence for almost twenty minutes before his phone rang. He startled so badly he almost spilled what was left of his coffee. He pounced on the phone when he saw Matt Callahan's name on the screen. He hit the speaker button so that Grace and Ian could hear too. "Did you and Duchess find something?"

"No, I took Duchess all around Greenland Park, but she didn't alert on Caleb's scent. Did you find anything at White Park?"

"No, but a witness claimed she saw a black Honda sedan there. Maybe you could take Duchess to check out the bathrooms?"

"I will, right after I give her a break. She'll go until she drops if I don't make her rest a bit."

"Please give her time to recover, especially since we may need her later. Even if Caleb and the kidnapper were at the park earlier, they weren't there when we drove through."

"Understood. I can try more parks too. I think there's another one in Brookland that may fit our criteria," Matt offered.

"Only if you think Duchess is up to it. I want her fresh if we experience a glitch with the exchange." Brady hid a wince when Grace shot him a stunned look. "It's better to be prepared for any possibility," he added, hoping to reassure her.

"Checking out just the restroom area of both White Park and the one in Brookland shouldn't be too much for her. I agree we want to be on alert in case something else comes through. Let me know if you hear anything more about the location of the exchange."

"I will. Thanks, Matt." He disconnected from the call, wondering if he should contact Lieutenant Krull, the day shift commander at the local precinct, to see if there was any new information from the tip line. Although he firmly believed Krull would call him if they had a viable lead.

He drained his coffee, feeling as if he was juggling too many balls at one time and risked dropping something important.

For the first time, he was at a loss as to how to prioritize. Normally, he didn't have this problem. But knowing Caleb was his son added an emotional connection.

One he couldn't ignore.

He abruptly stood and grabbed his phone. He called Marc Callahan, needing advice. His call went straight to voice mail, so he left his fellow agent a quick message to call him back.

"What do you need Marc for?" Grace asked as he dropped back into his chair.

"Nothing really." He didn't want to worry her about his sudden attack of self-doubt. She needed him to be confident. Working cases like this was his job, one he used to be good at. "Let's keep searching for a photo that matches our sketch."

"It's ten forty-five," Grace said. "Shouldn't the kidnapper call soon with a location for the exchange?"

"If he gives us too much time, we'll have the place staked out by dozens of undercover cops." He managed a smile. "He'll call, but probably closer to the deadline."

"The waiting is killing me," she whispered.

"Me too." He touched her hand, then turned back to the computer screen. He'd gone through three more names when he stumbled upon a Larry Abrams from Chicago who was in the right age group. He had a large family picture as his cover photo, so he blew it up on his screen to see better.

This Larry Abrams did not resemble the sketch, although the way he stood with his arm around his parents made him wonder if he wasn't the victim they were looking for. "Hey, Ian, see what you can find out about Larry Abrams from Chicago. His date of birth is November tenth of 1990."

"Give me a minute." Ian switched over to enter the information into the database. "I found his driver's license, but he doesn't have a car registered under his name."

It could be listed under his parents' names. "Dig deeper, will you? I'd like proof that his parents aren't the victims of the investment scheme. If not, I think we can cross him off our list as he has roughly a hundred pounds and different hair color than the perp in our sketch." Eliminating suspects wasn't as fun as finding the diamond in the sand, but it would allow them to switch their focus to other suspects.

"Yep, found them." Ian whistled under his breath. "Looks like they lost two million and change in the scam. I agree he's not our guy, though. No way does he match our sketch."

"Agreed." Brady tried not to sigh loud enough for Grace to hear. "It's good to know we can move on."

"There are so many possibilities," Grace said. "I don't think I'll ever find the right Dominic Powers."

"We will. I'll help you. You keep searching on Dominic Powers, and I'll use Nick. Oh, and exclude anyone over the age of fifty. That will also help narrow the list of suspects down."

"I used the age of fifty-five, but fifty works too," Ian said.

He'd only gone through a dozen names when Callahan returned his call. He scooped up the phone. "Please tell me you have something."

"I've been helping Lieutenant Krull go through the tips, and we just received a call from a witness claiming she saw them," Marc said. "At another fast-food joint if you can believe it."

"Where?" Brady was torn between drilling into social media posts and heading straight over to talk to the witness.

"It's a drive-through ice-cream and burger joint in Greenland." He could hear the sound of a car engine in the background. "I'm heading there now."

"We'll meet you there." He couldn't pass up the chance of interviewing a witness or maybe getting a glimpse of the car on a security camera. "Thanks, Marc."

"I'll keep digging into these names," Ian said. "I'll let you know if I'm able to eliminate another suspect from the list."

"Thanks." He reached for Grace's hand. "Let's go."

"Hold on." She hung back long enough to grab the laptop, clutching it to her chest without closing or logging off. "I'll work in the car."

He didn't mention that he had more faith in Ian's ability to find their suspect. It wasn't that he didn't trust Grace, he did. But she wasn't an investigator. Still, he wasn't about to argue. "That's fine."

"What was that about an ice-cream and burger place?" Grace asked as they headed outside.

The sun was warming the temperatures. He pushed up the sleeves of his sweatshirt, wishing he could change into something lighter. "That's where the witness claims she saw the guy in your sketch and Caleb."

"I'm glad he's taking the time to give Caleb something to eat." She slid into the passenger seat, keeping the computer on her lap. "I was afraid he'd avoid doing that after the breakfast incident."

"Keep in mind the kidnapper may not realize we have witnesses calling in sightings of him." Brady started the engine and pulled out of the parking lot. "I doubt he has kids of his own, so maybe he's underestimated the power of a mother's keen eye."

"You're probably right." She settled the laptop on her legs. "I'm so thankful for every person out there who took the time to call in a tip."

"Me too." He concentrated on driving, wishing now that he'd stayed at White Park rather than heading back to the office. Maybe it was better to stay out in the field, leaving Ian and others to work the case from their head-quarters.

As if he needed more proof as to how his being emotion-ally involved in this case was getting in the way. He felt like a yo-yo bouncing between clues. Maybe he should call Donovan and ask for Marc to be assigned as the lead.

"I found a guy named Dominic Powers in Chicago!" Grace's excited voice broke into his thoughts. "I can't see any other pictures of him, though. He has a cartoon image uploaded as his profile picture."

"Call Ian, give him the information." He didn't dare take his eyes off the road to look at the screen for himself.

Not when he was already pushing the speed limit. "He has better tech skills to dig into that stuff."

"Ah, okay. What number do I call?" She had her cell phone in hand.

He gave her the number, listening as she explained what she'd found to Ian. A few minutes later, she lowered her phone. "He found a Joe Custer living near the Illinois/Wisconsin state line. He's going to get both of their driver's license photos for us."

"That's good news." Adrenaline surged as he realized they were starting to gain traction on this case. As the clock now read 11:22 a.m., he knew they needed every lead they could get.

He hadn't heard from Rhy about the ransom but decided not to worry about it. Rhy would let him know if there was a problem. In the meantime, he hoped they'd find Caleb before the one o'clock exchange.

In a location as yet to be determined.

The ice-cream/burger restaurant was up ahead. It was a popular place, so he wasn't surprised to see it was busy. The parking lot was almost completely full of cars, and for a moment, he wondered if the witness had made a mistake.

Spying Marc Callahan's SUV, he pulled into the parking lot. The only empty spot was on the other end of the lot, so he drove that way. In the rearview, he saw Marc Callahan jogging over to meet with them.

"Witness's name is Martha Logan," Marc said as they got out of the car. "She's an employee here. I see a couple of cameras, too, so maybe we'll get video of this guy and his license plate."

Grace left the laptop in the car. Together they went inside the busy restaurant. They must have looked official because a young woman wearing a polyester uniform and a hairnet slipped out from behind the counter to meet them.

"Hi, I'm Martha." Her eyes were wide. "I am absolutely convinced I served the kidnapper two small burgers and an ice-cream cone."

"Start at the beginning," Marc suggested. "What time was this?"

She pulled her phone from her pocket. "Twelve minutes ago. I tried to stall, but he didn't wait for his change. He grabbed the food and told the little boy that he needed to behave to get the ice-cream cone. Oh, and the boy wasn't wearing the Avengers pajamas either. He had a worn T-shirt on that was too big and shorts that covered his knees."

The kidnapper had changed Caleb's clothes? It was a smart thing to do, but he wondered where he'd gotten the items. Possibly at a secondhand clothing store. "Did the little boy say anything?" Brady asked. "Indicate in any way that he was being held against his will?"

"No, but he did this motion with his hands." She demonstrated what she meant, making a fist with one hand and placing it in the palm of the other hand. Then she brought both up to her chin. "He did this twice," she emphasized. "I knew that meant he was in trouble."

Brady frowned. "I don't understand."

"It's sign language," Grace spoke up excitedly. "We teach some sign language to the little kids at the day care center so we can understand what they want. It's easier for them to learn that than to say certain words. This sign"—she repeated the movements Martha had done—"means help."

"Yes, I learned some sign language babysitting for some little kids in the neighborhood," Martha said. "It took me a minute to figure it out, and by then, the driver had pulled away."

"We need to see your video of the car he was driving." Brady tried to contain his excitement. He was thrilled his son had managed to signal for help, and even more happy that this Martha had recognized the sign-language gesture he'd performed. "Please, we need that license plate number."

"I told my manager you would, this way." Martha led them behind the counter to a very small office located off to the side of the kitchen. "This is Jeremy, my manager. These are the FBI agents who'd like to see the video."

"I have it pulled up for you." The manager was young but eager to please. He turned his laptop computer around so the three of them could see the screen. "It's a little blurry, but it's the best I can do."

"We'll take anything you have," Marc assured him. "Thanks for your cooperation."

"Of course." Jeremy pressed the play button, and they all watched as a dark car pulled up to the drive-through window. The angle of the camera was such that it was difficult to see Caleb in the back seat. Even the profile view of the perp's face was grainier than he'd have liked. But the resemblance to the sketch was uncanny.

The guy handed over a twenty-dollar bill, took the food, and quickly drove off. There was a very blurred image of a little boy in the back seat wearing a dirty white shirt, and then he was gone.

"Stop it there!" Brady said urgently. Jeremy did as he was told. "I can see the license plate, EPR 708."

Marc lifted his phone to his ear. "Lieutenant Krull? We need a BOLO on a four-door black Honda with the following Wisconsin license plate." He rattled off the three letters and the three digits.

Brady knew they'd find this guy now that they had his license plate number! He wanted to hug Martha for her quick thinking but wrapped his arm around Grace's shoulders instead.

This was exactly the break in the case that they needed!

CHAPTER EIGHT

"I don't like this," the mean man said. "I think that woman stared at you too long and took note of this car."

Caleb was finishing his ice-cream cone, so he didn't say anything. He'd been afraid the mean man would notice what he was doing when he'd used the help sign-language sign to get the woman's attention. The way she'd stared at him had made him worry she had no idea what he was trying to say.

"I need to change out the license plate." The mean man was still talking to himself. Caleb frowned. If he did something with the license plate, would that make it harder for his mom and the police to find him?

After talking to his mom on the phone, he'd felt better knowing she was looking for him. He'd cried when the mean man grabbed the phone away, and he had wanted to kick him. But he didn't. Right after that, the mean man took his Avengers pajamas away and made him wear these old stinky clothes that didn't fit.

Now the mean man looked upset again.

Caleb frowned when he noticed they were driving

through a wooded area. It looked like the park where he'd gotten out to use the bathroom, although there were more people out now. Maybe the mean man would let him go to the bathroom again?

"That could work," the mean man said. Then he smiled in a way that made Caleb worry. "Yeah, that's what I'll do."

The mean man pulled over to the side of the road, behind a long line of other cars that were parked there. Then he shut off the engine and turned to glare at him. "Don't try anything or I'll smack you, understand?"

"Yes." Caleb tried not to be afraid. He knew he needed to be brave until his mom could come find him.

The mean man got out of the car, slammed the door, then pulled something out of the trunk. Caleb thought he saw a tool in the mean man's hands, but then he was gone.

Caleb was alone in the car for the first time since the mean man had taken him from his bedroom. He quickly unbuckled the belt holding him in the booster seat and climbed into the front.

Peering out the window, he didn't see the mean man. What was he was doing? Caleb had no idea, but the woods were located just a few yards away.

Without taking the time to think it through, he opened the car door and slid out. Then he ran across the grass toward the woods as fast as he could despite the too-big shoes the mean man had given him.

While hoping the mean man wouldn't know he was gone until he was far, far away.

GRACE CLUNG to Brady as he led her back to the SUV. Seeing Caleb's blurred image provided a renewed energy.

He hadn't looked mistreated from what she could tell, although it had been a shock to see that he wasn't wearing his Avengers pajamas.

Of course, the kidnapper would make Caleb wear different clothes. It may have even been done when they stopped at the park restroom where Duchess had tracked her son's scent.

"How soon will the police find the black Honda?" She had been glad her identification of the vehicle had been correct. Knowing the vehicle's license plate should help track the kidnapper down.

"Marc made sure that every law enforcement agency in the entire metropolitan area is on alert for the Honda." Brady gave her a gentle squeeze before opening the SUV passenger door for her. "We'll find him."

"Before the one o'clock deadline?" She knew better than to ask for something Brady couldn't tell her. Having all the cops on alert for one specific vehicle was more than they'd had before. "Never mind, I know you can't answer that." She blew out a breath. "It just feels like we're so close, yet so is the time the kidnapper set for the exchange."

"Waiting is the hardest part." Brady flashed a reassuring smile. "Let's put our faith in God's hands."

Way easier said than done, but she didn't voice her concern. Especially since she'd been leaning on prayer throughout this ordeal. She silently vowed to continue praying for Caleb's safekeeping.

Maybe she didn't deserve God's grace, but surely her son did.

Their son.

She wouldn't have any idea where Caleb was at all without Brady's skills and support. The fact that he was being so kind to her after the way she'd treated him was also amazing.

Seven years ago, she'd loved him. Now she found herself impressed with the man he'd become. He'd been admirable even back then. Now he was even more so.

In truth, Caleb deserved a father like Brady. No matter how difficult it would be for her, she'd make sure Brady had plenty of time to get to know his son.

Once they had him back from the kidnapper.

"Where are we headed?" The brief spurt of energy began to fade. "Back to the office?"

"Not yet. I hate to be far away if the kidnapper's vehicle is found." Brady shrugged. "I'll drive around for a bit; he can't be that far from here."

She was relieved they weren't going back and opened the laptop computer. "I'll keep searching for Dominic Powers." She frowned at the black screen. "Although I need the log-in information."

Brady called Ian, who answered on the first ring. "I'm still going through the list of Joe, Joey, and Josephs," he said in a defensive tone. "The guy on the border isn't the one we were looking for."

"I know, that's fine. Give Grace the log-in information for the laptop, will you? She wants to work as we drive."

Grace quickly typed in the information Ian provided. "Don't go memorizing that, okay? Otherwise I'll have to change it when you get back."

"I won't. Thanks, Ian."

"You'll have to change it anyway," Brady pointed out. "I don't suppose there's any other information from the investigation?"

"Not yet." Ian sounded apologetic. "I'll bug the cell companies again if they don't get back to me soon."

"That would be great, thanks. We'll be in touch." Brady ended the call.

"It seems like we should have more to go on," she said as she began searching through the social media site again. "Considering how many professionals are working the case."

"If this guy had a criminal background, it would be easier," Brady said dryly. His phone rang again, and the name on the screen in the dashboard was Rhy. "Hey, bro, what's the word?"

"We've got the ransom," Rhy said with satisfaction. "Bax came through for us, although it was no easy task. I think he had to use all of his connections to get this money extricated from the various funds he had them in. But the entire five million will be ready to be transferred when we know Caleb is safe."

"I'm impressed," Brady said.

"I have the second mortgage paperwork going through the banking system, too, but I don't think we'll be able to get the funds by the deadline," Rhy added. "It's only a drop in the bucket of the five-million demand, but I wanted us to contribute something. So far Bax has refused to take it, but we'll worry about that later. I have to admit, the kidnapper using an offshore account is smart. It won't be easy to make the transfer, get Caleb back, then find a way to track the money to get the funds back."

"I know, we'll need to think this through," Brady agreed solemnly. "I can't stand the idea of Bax losing this much money."

"He said he doesn't mind as long as we get Caleb back."

Grace didn't personally know Bax, but she wanted to give him a big hug and a kiss of gratitude.

"That's nice of him, but we'll find a way to protect his

funds." The expression on Brady's face reflected his determination. "We don't have a location yet where this guy is going to allow us to take Caleb. I'm assuming he must have a computer, too, to track the transfer of ransom funds into his designated account."

"That seems logical," Rhy agreed. "If we could get the ISP address, we can try tracking him that way."

"I wish," Brady said with a sigh. "So far he hasn't given us much of anything to go on. Although we do have a license plate number."

"I saw that, good work." Rhy's voice rang with satisfaction. "All officers in every precinct have been put on alert to grab this guy."

"That's the plan. Thanks, Rhy. Stay close to your phone, as soon as we hear from this perp again, we'll let you know."

"Understood. Just as an FYI, Bax is sticking with me too. Thankfully, he's not in court today."

"Great. I'll be in touch soon." Brady disconnected from the call.

"I cannot believe Bax offered up his personal funds for this," Grace said. "And really, as wonderful as that is, what is this kidnapper thinking? How did he expect me to get this money? We live in a single-bedroom apartment."

"He must assume your brother still has funds stashed away somewhere." Brady held her gaze for a moment. "Are you sure he doesn't?"

She frowned. "How would I know? He's in federal prison. It's not like I can walk in and ask him."

"No, but it is something we can dig into later. I would like to think the SEC did that already, but it can't hurt. Not that losing an entire retirement fund justifies kidnapping, but I feel for the victims."

"I do too." She hated knowing what her brother had done. "But nothing justifies scaring a six-year-old boy. Nothing!"

"I know." He reached over to take her hand. It was surprising how often he did that, as if maybe he needed some support too. "We'll find him. And we know he's been given breakfast and lunch."

"That and seeing him in the video are the only things holding me together," she confided. "I'd be a bigger wreck if I thought this guy had hurt Caleb. Or worse."

"He won't. We'll find him."

She desperately wanted to believe him. She continued working through the social media sites, but it was difficult to concentrate. By the time they identified this guy, it would be time for him to call with more information.

Now that they had the ransom set, thanks to Bax's generosity, she wished he'd just call and give them the information.

She couldn't wait to hold Caleb in her arms once this nightmare was over.

DRIVING around looking for the black Honda probably wasn't the best use of his time, but Brady couldn't help himself. Not when he knew without a shadow of a doubt this kidnapper had been at the ice-cream and burger place just twenty minutes ago.

He circled the block, then went around another block. As he continued driving, he realized they weren't that far from Greenland Park.

Matt and Duchess had already searched the place, but that didn't mean their perp hadn't headed over after getting an early lunch. But before he could turn to head that way, his phone rang again. Ian's name flashed on the screen.

"We have a possible phone number," Ian said in lieu of a greeting. "Obviously, it's a cheap disposable phone, but we ran it through the system, and it was purchased at a discount store not far from the day care center owned by Ms. Ramsey." There was a pause before Ian continued. "Here's the address. I thought you'd want to head over there ASAP."

"We do, thanks." He repeated the address in his head as he turned to head in the opposite direction. "Are you familiar with the discount store Ian mentioned?"

"Yes, I shop there all the time." She shivered. "It's creepy to know the kidnapper went there too."

"He must have staked out your day care center for a few days," Brady mused. "Longer than you realized."

"I try to stay vigilant because of the children." She ran her fingers through her hair. "It hurts to know that my son was taken because of my inattentiveness."

"That's not the reason, Grace. You know that this guy is looking for restitution for losing a retirement fund." He didn't want her to keep beating herself up over this. "How could you expect that to happen?"

She didn't answer, her gaze pensive. Finally, she said, "You're right, no mother can expect their child to be taken. Even teaching our kids about stranger danger didn't help in this case. It takes Caleb a few minutes to wake up; he was probably already out of the apartment and in the car by then."

The kidnapper had done that part right. Using the old *help me find my puppy* trick may not have worked with Caleb.

"Turn left at the next light." He noticed she'd closed the

laptop computer, maybe realizing this phone number might give them the name of their UNSUB quicker than searching endless variations of names. "Do they track serial numbers on these phones?"

"The numbers are listed on the receipt." He paused, then added, "If he used cash, we may not get very far."

Grace sighed. "Well, this is fruitless, then. I'm sure he used cash."

"Maybe not. He's going through cash with the hotel and fast-food places. Don't underestimate the possibility of his using a credit or debit card."

"It's going on noon," she said. "Why hasn't he called back yet?"

He knew she was talking out loud rather than expecting an answer. He parked in the discount store lot and pushed out of the SUV. "Let's go. I have a good feeling about this, Grace. If we can get this guy's number, we'll call him about the exchange while tracking his current location."

"I pray you're right." She hurried along beside him. "I keep telling myself that no matter what happens, we'll have our son back within the hour."

"Our son," he echoed, glancing at her. "I like the sound of that."

"Me too." She caught his hand. "You've been a rock, Brady. Thank you for being such a great FBI agent. We wouldn't be this far in the investigation if not for you."

"It's a team effort." Her kind words meant a lot to him. They didn't take back the fact that she'd kept Caleb a secret from him, but going through this ordeal together had brought them closer.

In some ways, it was as if the seven-year gap between them hadn't happened.

Something to discuss once they had Caleb back. For

now, he planned to follow up on every possible lead. Until they got the call about the exchange.

Brady flashed his creds to the first employee he saw. "I'm Special Agent Finnegan. I need to speak with your manager as soon as possible."

The young man's eyes widened in shock. "Ah, sure." He reached up to push a button on his headset. "Um, Ms. Wellington? There's an FBI agent here to talk to you."

Several customers walking by stopped to gape. Brady ignored them, his gaze sweeping the store for the manager.

A round woman who appeared to be in her late fifties hurried over from where the cashiers were located. "I'm Mary Wellington. What can I do for you?"

"Special Agent Finnegan," he repeated, giving her a moment to see his creds before sliding the pack back into his pocket. "You sold a disposable phone here four days ago. I want to find out who bought it."

"Do you have a time frame in mind?" She frowned. "We sell a lot of phones."

"Can you pull up all phone transactions?" He wasn't sure what technical skills this woman possessed. "Or can you pull up all transactions for that day? I can always send the entire list to my office so our IT expert can go through it."

"Let me see what I can do." She turned and gestured for them to join her. "My office is this way. Oh, uh, shouldn't you have a warrant or something?"

He nodded. "Yes, I'll have one faxed over ASAP. A missing six-year-old boy's life is at stake. We appreciate your cooperation."

"I have a five-year-old grandson." She frowned and waved a hand. "I'll get you whatever you need, Agent

Finnegan. People who steal children are the lowest scum of the earth."

"I couldn't agree more," Grace muttered.

"Thank you." He wished all witnesses were so helpful. He used his phone to get the search warrant sent over, then followed the manager.

Her office was cramped, but she logged into the computer and began working. "Four days ago, here we are." She looked up at him. "We sell a lot of products in a day, it would really help if you had a time frame."

"I don't have one, sorry. If you can't separate the list by item, then print everything out for me."

"Wait a minute, I think I can run a report of all electronics that were sold." She worked as she spoke. "Yep, here you go. It looks like we only sold one phone that day." She printed out a sheet of paper and handed it to him. "Does that help you?"

He scanned the list until he saw the phone sale. His pulse spiked when he saw a phone number with a local area code, along with the last four digits of a credit card number. "He used a credit card; I need his name and the entire card number."

"Hmm." She frowned and stared at her computer screen. "I'm not sure how to get that information."

"May I try?" It was all he could do not to wrench the woman from her seat so he could take over. "Please? It's really important."

"Sure." She shrugged and rose to her feet, scooting out of his way. "Have at it."

"How are you going to figure out their system?" Grace asked.

He wasn't as much of a tech whiz as Ian, but he knew his way around basic operating systems. He doubted the discount store used anything super fancy. He took a moment to familiarize himself with the various tabs of the spreadsheet she'd pulled up, then searched for a transaction detail page.

"How often do you get to see your grandson?" Grace asked.

"Every week or so," Mary Wellington said. "If two weeks go by, I go into grandson withdrawal," she joked. "I only live ten minutes from my son and his wife, which helps."

"That sounds so wonderful. My parents live in Florida, they don't get to see their grandson that often," Grace said. "Mostly on holidays."

He tried to stay focused on finding the credit card information from the phone-buying transaction, but listening to Grace made him realize that her parents being so far away meant she had little to no support in raising Caleb. No one to help her when he was sick or when she simply needed a break.

Granted, he should have been the one to do that, but it still bothered him.

He should be glad she hadn't moved to Florida with Caleb or he'd never see his son. Or he would have to give up seeing so much of his family to move down there to be with them.

Enough. This wasn't important, finding the name of their kidnapper was. He poked around in the system until he found the transaction details he was looking for.

"Got it," he said. "Name on the credit card is Parker Hall." He wondered who in the world Parker Hall was since he wasn't one of their suspects, but he quickly printed the page. "This is exactly what we needed, Ms. Wellington. Thank you so much."

"I hope you catch him very soon," she said, following them out of her office.

"We will now that we have this." He pulled out his phone and dialed Ian. "Our UNSUB has a name, Parker Hall. I know he's not on our list of suspects, but he has to be linked to the investment scheme in some way. Find everything you can about him, Ian. I mean everything. He has Caleb."

"On it," Ian said, keys clicking in the background. "You're right, he's not one of the investors who'd lost money in the scam. I'll call you back as soon as I have something more."

"Thanks." He pocketed his phone and drew Grace outside. "We have his name and his license plate number. This is good news, Grace. We're getting close."

"I believe you." Her smile didn't quite meet her eyes. "It's weird that Parker Hall wasn't on your suspect list. And I'm worried because it's five minutes past noon, and he still hasn't called."

"I'll call Hall directly once we're in the car." He didn't want the outside noise around them to give their location away. Especially since there were train tracks not far from the store. "Maybe using his name will scare him into giving us the location early." Or in giving up Caleb and this scheme to get the money back altogether.

"Wait." She grabbed his arm. "What if he hurts Caleb? Maybe we should give him just a little more time."

He opened the car door for her, then went around to slide in behind the wheel. "I'm calling him now but need to make sure Ian can help pinpoint his location." He called Ian back with his plan, then put Ian on hold to make the call to Parker Hall's cell phone.

The call wasn't answered, and there was no voice mailbox set up to leave a message.

He blew out a breath, realizing he should have expected this. He clicked back to Ian. "Never mind, his phone isn't on. We'll try again in ten to fifteen minutes."

"That's fine. There are a couple of Parker Halls in Chicago, so I'm still digging to find the right one," Ian informed him. "I'm sure one of these guys will match our sketch. Once we have his address, we'll get a search warrant for his home."

"That's good. We'll want cops staked out at his place of residence too." He didn't expect Parker Hall to head home until after the exchange since Chicago was a ninety-minute drive on a good day, but he wanted all bases covered. "Anything else?"

"Not yet," Ian sounded testy. "I only got two hands, you know?"

"Yeah, never mind, I'll call Donovan to let him know we have a name to go with the Amber Alert. I'd like to know if Donovan heard from the agents who went to speak with Adam Ramsey in the federal penitentiary too." He paused, then added, "Thanks again, Ian."

"I'll call when I have news," Ian said.

He lowered his phone and tried not to feel dejected. They'd gotten the kidnapper's name and his vehicle. If this wasn't enough for the local police to get him into custody, he didn't know what would be.

"Why does it always feel like everything we do is never enough?" Grace asked.

He wasn't sure how to answer that. He called Donovan and brought his boss up to speed. "Two things, I want the Amber Alert issued with the perp's full name, and I would like to know what, if anything, the agents learned from visiting Adam Ramsey in prison."

"I'll take care of the Amber Alert," Donovan agreed. "But the Chicago office informed me Ramsey didn't have additional information to share. He claims he doesn't know anything about the kidnapping."

Brady wished he could have done the interview with Grace's brother himself. He had a hard time believing Adam didn't know anything. "Okay, thanks."

"I hope you find this jerk, and soon," Donovan said, sounding more like the boss he knew.

"Me too." He no sooner hung up from the call when his phone rang again. This time the caller was Marc Callahan. "Hey, Marc. Perp's name is Parker Hall, so far he's an unknown. Not one of our top suspects or on the list of investors who'd gotten scammed."

"Good to know, but you're going to want to get here to this young couple's house in Greenland," Marc said. "They called in a stolen license plate."

"And that's significant, why?" He started the engine and put the phone in his hands-free holder.

"I have a feeling your buddy Parker Hall stole a license plate to stay under the radar," Marc explained. "Their car isn't a Honda, but it's a black four-door Ford sedan. I don't like coincidences."

"We're on our way." Brady didn't like coincidences either. It appeared Parker Hall was smarter than they'd given him credit for. Brady had hoped to have him in custody by now.

They were running out of time to grab him before the exchange.

CHAPTER NINE

Caleb had run into the woods, hoping to stay hidden from the mean man. He tripped over a log, falling to his hands and knees. The stupid shoes the mean man had given him were too big. He wanted to cry, but he knew he needed to keep going. To stay hidden from the mean man.

He didn't know how to get home. His mommy always told him if he was lost to find a policeman. Or a mommy or daddy to get help. Not stranger danger, like the mean man. But a mommy or daddy with a kid.

But first he had to hide from the mean man.

He crawled behind a tree, rubbing his scraped knee. He sniffled, trying hard not to cry. He wanted his mommy really bad.

"Caleb, get back here right now!"

The mean man's voice made him shrink farther behind the tree. No! He didn't want the mean man to find him! He needed to hide! Caleb looked behind him but didn't see the mean man. He decided to keep running. He was fast. The other kids at the day care told him so. He took off, trying not to trip over the stupid shoes as he went farther into the woods.

After stopping to catch his breath, he saw the playground. There weren't any other kids playing there that he could see, but he knew it would be the best place to find other mommies and daddies.

He peeked behind him one more time to make sure the mean man wasn't following, then ran again. Leaving the shade of the woods was hard, but he went straight to the jungle gym. There was a small area beneath the slide, so he crawled inside, squishing himself into the space to make himself as small as possible.

Caleb listened but didn't hear the mean man calling him anymore. He didn't think the mean man could see him. Caleb stayed hidden in the small space behind the slide, hoping the mean man would give up and go away.

He closed his eyes and waited for other mommies and daddies to come and help him.

WHO IN THE world was Parker Hall? Grace turned the name over and over in her mind, trying to figure out why it sounded even vaguely familiar. It wasn't one of the names on the suspect list, which she found strange. It made her fear that he'd been hired by someone on the suspect list to do the kidnapping.

Had she met this Parker Hall at one time? The guy's face in the sketch didn't look at all familiar, but the name nagged at her.

She was so lost in thought it took her a moment to realize Brady had made a sharp turn to head in the opposite direction. "Wait, what's going on?"

Brady looked surprised at her question. "I thought you overheard me talking to Marc Callahan. A young couple living in Greenland called in a stolen license plate. They own a black Ford sedan. We're heading over to talk to them."

"You think the kidnapper stole it to use on the Honda?"

"It's one theory," Brady admitted. "We won't know for sure until we find the stolen plate."

She'd thought things would be easier when they had the kidnapper's name, but she felt as lost as ever. It didn't help knowing his name was Parker Hall. Not when this man could be anywhere in the city.

Why did that name bother her?

The stress of this nightmare was wearing her down. She was overreacting to the guy's name. As far as she knew, she wasn't friends or acquaintances with any of her brother's victims.

She rubbed her gritty eyes and tried not to fall apart. All she wanted was to find Caleb. Was that too much to ask? She didn't think so, but maybe she was being punished for her poor decisions.

Too many to count.

"That must be them up ahead." Brady's comment interrupted her unhelpful thoughts. She squinted against the bright sunlight. A young couple stood outside next to their black sedan. Marc Callahan had gotten there first and was already speaking with the couple.

When Brady stopped the car, she jumped out and hurried over to hear the discussion. She was acutely aware of Brady coming up beside her.

"This is FBI Agent Brady Finnegan and Grace Ramsey. Brady, the owners of the Ford sedan are Sarah and Jeff Cole." Marc made brief introductions. "They were explaining to me how they'd taken their lunch break at Greenland Park. They sat at a picnic table to eat, and when they finished, returned to their vehicle. It was only when they arrived at home that they noticed their license plate was missing."

"Nothing like this has ever happened to us before," Sarah said, looking worried.

"We appreciate your cooperation," Brady assured her. "Can you describe where exactly you were parked?"

"We entered on the south side of the park, driving maybe a quarter mile before pulling over to the side of the road," Jeff explained. "We were at the picnic table roughly fifteen or twenty minutes before we came back."

"Yes, we usually only take a thirty-minute break," Sarah agreed. "We both work from home and thought the change of scenery would be nice."

Grace noticed Marc took notes as they spoke. She was glad they'd noticed the missing plate and called it in, but she didn't see how this was going to help them find Caleb."

"Did you see a black Honda or the man in the Amber Alert sketch?" Brady asked.

"No, we would have called into the tip line if we had, right, hon?" Jeff put his arm around his wife's shoulders.

"Yes, of course. You really think the kidnapper stole our plate to use on his car?" Sarah asked.

"We don't know, but it's one theory," Marc said. "Especially now that the Amber Alert has gone out with the license plate number." Marc turned toward them. "I put a BOLO out on the stolen plate number too. Hopefully, someone will spot it, especially since they're already looking for the black Honda."

"Thanks," Brady said.

"Terrible news about that missing boy," Jeff said with a frown.

Grace held herself together with an effort. This young couple didn't appear to have kids of their own, and she hoped they would never have to experience this nightmare. She didn't say anything, sensing it was best to have the questions coming from the two FBI agents.

"If you think of anything else, will you please call me?" Marc Callahan held out his business card. "It's important we find this little boy."

"Of course." Sarah's gaze flashed to Grace. "I'm sorry for what you're going through."

"Thank you." She tried to smile but failed.

Brady took her hand, gently tugging her back toward the car. Marc joined them.

"I was hoping to get more from the Coles," Marc admitted. "Although they gave us a good time frame to work with."

"How does that help me?" Grace winced, realizing her question came out sounding like a complaint. "I don't mean to sound negative, but we are no closer to finding Caleb. And the deadline for the exchange is only forty-five minutes away!" Panic rose in the back of her throat, choking her. "Why hasn't Parker Hall called? What's taking so long?"

"I know things haven't been moving as quickly as you'd like. But we are making progress." Brady tightened his grip on her hand. "Parker Hall's ransom demand indicates his motive is money. He will call."

That's what he kept saying, but deep down, she was having trouble believing it. The not knowing about her son's whereabouts was killing her.

"Does Donovan know our UNSUB has a name?" Marc asked.

"Yes. He's asking the team to crossmatch our list of suspects with Parker Hall. He was either hired by one of the victims or is close with one."

"There's no way they'll find a connection before one o'clock," Grace protested. "Is there something else we can do? Someplace we can look?"

"If Hall stole the license plate from Greenland Park, I highly doubt he'd hang around," Brady said. He hesitated, then added, "It may be time for us to head back to the FBI office. We need to be ready for the exchange call."

It was on the tip of her tongue to ask what they would do if the call didn't come in, but she held back. All this negativity wasn't helping. She needed to think positive. To remember that Parker Hall may be the monster who kidnapped their son, but he had also fed the boy two meals, giving him a chocolate shake and ice cream.

Something she doubted ever happened in other kidnapping cases.

"Grace? Are you okay with that plan?" Brady asked.

"I'd rather keep driving around to find him," she answered honestly. "But I know that's not the best use of our time."

"I feel the same way, but we need to be prepared for whatever instructions Hall is planning to give us," Brady said.

"Okay, fine." What else could she say? She'd gone to Brady early on because she'd trusted him.

She couldn't afford to stop trusting him now.

"I'll stay in touch," Marc said. "I plan to drive through the park just to be sure we didn't miss something."

"Call me if you find anything," Brady said with a nod. "Ready, Grace?"

She pulled from his grasp and headed for the passenger-side door. Her frazzled nerves made her skin feel like it was on fire. She was hot and cold at the same time, almost as if she had a fever.

The impact of more than twelve hours of stress. And she could only hope and pray that by one o'clock, they'd have Caleb back.

Please, Lord, please? Bring Caleb home!

BRADY COULD TELL Grace was close to losing faith. And he understood why she felt that way. It wasn't easy to keep going when every clue in the case didn't get them any closer to finding their son.

Once they were settled in the SUV and on the road, he called his oldest brother, Rhy.

"I saw you have the kidnapper's name. Do you also have a meeting place to make the exchange?" Rhy asked.

"Not yet." He cast a worried glance at Grace. "I'm sure Parker Hall will call soon. I'm looking for any help you and the rest of the Finnegans can give me with digging into Parker Hall. He wasn't on the top of the suspect list and isn't one of the investors who'd lost money to Adam Ramsey either."

"A hired kidnapper?" Rhy asked.

"I'm leaning that way, yes. It's the only thing that makes sense." Brady noticed Grace was twisting her fingers again, so he reached over to take her hand. "I'm hoping Hall has some connection to one of the scam victims. Our tech specialist is working hard to find his home address and other personal information, but I feel like the more people involved with finding this guy, the better our chances are of finding him."

"I get it." The tapping sound of fingers on keys came through the speaker. "I'll see what I can dig up. Are you sure Grace doesn't know Parker Hall?"

"I don't remember meeting a man named Parker Hall," Grace spoke up. "There is something vaguely familiar about the name, but I can't remember when or where I might have heard it."

Brady looked at her in surprise. "Maybe the father of a child at your day care center?"

Her brow furrowed. "No. There aren't any kids with the last name of Hall."

"Is there a possibility one of the families using your day care center are victims of your brother's scam?" Rhy asked. "Maybe without the same last name of Hall? Like a more distant relative? Aunts, uncles, or cousins? I only ask because it's a logical place to start."

"Again, not that I know of." Grace tightened her grip on his hand. "I mean, what are the chances of that? I purposefully came to Ravenswood because it's a small, quiet community compared to Chicago. There aren't any wealthy people living around me. My day care kids come from lower-income families. A couple of them get vouchers from the state."

"Could be they are low income now because of the lost income from the investment scam," Brady mused. He gestured to the computer. "Go through that list of investors again, see if any names jump out at you."

Grace opened the computer and logged in using Ian's credentials. "I will, but I find it hard to believe that someone moved to Ravenswood, enrolled a child in my day care as a front to setting up a kidnapping. It's not logical."

"Kidnappers are rarely logical," Brady said. "They are

focused solely on what they believe is the quickest way to get what they want. In this case, five million dollars."

"While underestimating how quickly and urgently law enforcement will mobilize all resources to find a missing child," Rhy agreed.

"We haven't found him yet," Grace murmured.

"We will." Brady hated to see her so dejected. "Rhy, I have Ian cross-checking Parker Hall with the victims of the scam. What do you think about cross-checking his name with Grace's list of day care families?"

"I like it. Grace? Can you email me the list?" Rhy asked.

"I—uh, sure. Just a minute. I need to log into my email associated with my website."

Brady navigated traffic as Grace worked. A minute later, she asked, "Rhy, are you still there? I have the file."

"Yep. Send it to me electronically." He rattled off his email address. "I'll get right on this."

"Thanks, I appreciate that." He ended the call.

Grace was silent as she worked, which gave him time to review what they'd learned. The latest theory was that Parker Hall had kidnapped Caleb, likely to retrieve money he'd lost in Grace's brother's investment scam. He was driving around with Caleb and knew the authorities were closing in, so he'd stolen the Coles's license plate to bide time until the exchange could be made.

He decided to try Parker Hall's phone number again. When he hit the recent call button, there was only one ring before the call ended.

No answer and still no voice mailbox set up.

"Should I try with my phone?" Grace asked.

"Sure, go ahead."

She pulled her phone from her pocket and punched in

the numbers on the console. After a long moment, Grace sighed. "Still no answer."

"I'm sure Hall is purposefully keeping his phone off until he needs to use it."

"Yeah, I guess." Grace slid the phone back into her pocket.

Eyeing the dashboard clock, he swallowed hard upon realizing there was less than thirty minutes before the designated deadline.

A tingle of unease slid down his spine. Parker Hall was cutting it close. He honestly expected to hear from the kidnapper by now. Not that he planned to mention his concerns to Grace. She needed him to be strong and confident.

Yet doubts plagued him. What if he was wrong about this? What if the motive was to keep them busy searching for Caleb while Hall whisked him out of the state?

Out of the country?

He drew in a deep breath, striving to remain calm. Hall had been spotted at two fast-food restaurants. If he'd planned to skip town, he'd have done so by now.

Wouldn't he?

Seeing the FBI office building, he turned, then pulled into the parking lot. Grace glanced up from the computer screen when he stopped and shifted the SUV into park. "I haven't found anyone that sounds remotely familiar."

"Thanks for double-checking." He turned off the car engine. "Let's go inside. Maybe Ian has found something."

She closed the computer and tucked it under her arm. He led the way inside, going straight to the conference room where he suspected Ian was still working.

"Hey, Brady," Ian greeted him. "I've pulled up three different Parker Halls. This guy is the only one who looks like the sketch." Ian turned the screen to face him. "I'm thinking he must have dyed his hair brown."

He and Grace crowded close. "That's him, I'm sure of it." He glanced at Grace who nodded in agreement. "His DL has a Chicago address."

"Yeah, I'm sending this to the agents in Chicago to see if they can find him." Ian gestured to the screen. "I haven't gotten a hit off my cross-check of Hall with the investment victims yet. Looks like I'll have to dig deeper."

"There isn't time," Grace protested. "Parker Hall will be calling with a location to make the exchange any minute!"

"I'll keep working while we wait." Ian's gaze held sympathy. "I'll be ready when he calls."

"Waiting is horrible." Grace dropped into a chair and listlessly opened the laptop. "I can't stand it."

"Going through the list should help take your mind off it." He gently squeezed her shoulders.

She gazed up at him for a moment, then sat up straighter and logged in. He was about to do the same when he decided to check in with Donovan. Rather than leaving Grace alone this close to the deadline, he stepped away and called his boss. Keeping his voice low so Grace wouldn't overhear, he asked, "Please tell me you have an update from Chicago."

"I wish I could." Donovan sounded frustrated too. "The Hall residence is empty. Agents at the scene informed me it appears as if he hasn't been there in a few days. They're going to canvass the area to get more information on how long he's been gone, as well as searching the place for any key information, but so far it's not looking good."

"I was afraid of that." Brady swallowed a groan. They weren't gaining the ground they needed to find Caleb!

"Thanks, boss." He disconnected from the call and turned to find Grace's worried gaze resting on him. He tried to smile reassuringly. "My Chicago colleagues are searching Hall's home. I'm sure they'll find something to help."

"Are you?" Grace's expression indicated she did not believe him. "It's ten minutes to one. Parker Hall should have called by now."

Brady silently agreed. This idiot was cutting things close. Too close. He moved closer to the conference room table. "Maybe he's trying to find a place with good internet access to transfer the funds."

"Shouldn't he have been doing that earlier? He's had Caleb for hours. Thirteen long hours!" Grace's voice broke, then she gathered herself together. "No. Something is wrong, Brady. I have a bad feeling about this."

It was a concern he shared, although he did his best not to show it. "Any of those names sound familiar?"

"Not yet." With a heavy sigh, she turned her attention back to the computer. He paced the room, trying to come up with another avenue to explore. A clue as to where Hall may have been staying low with Caleb.

There were dozens of police officers out on the streets, searching for the Honda with the original license number or the stolen plate. It was maddening that no one had found it yet. He reached for his phone. "Marc? We need access to the cameras posted on all intersections. I find it impossible to believe Parker Hall has been able to avoid every camera in the city."

"Yeah, I've been thinking about that too. The problem is that a lot of intersection cameras don't work well, if at all, but I can try checking those that are closest to his last-known location," Marc said. "Give me a few minutes and I'll call you back."

Brady glanced over his shoulder at Grace and lowered his voice. "Thanks, Marc. We're running out of time. We have not heard a peep from Hall."

"I understand, Brady. Stay tuned." Marc ended the call.

Brady resumed pacing. He believed in God and had prayed nonstop since the little boy had been taken from his bed. Since learning Caleb was his son.

But it was more and more difficult not to wallow in despair. To give up on the idea that God was watching over Caleb.

His gaze landed again on the clock. Five minutes to one. Five minutes until the designated deadline set by Parker Hall himself.

Grace was right, something had gone wrong with the original plan. But what? Had the person who'd hired Hall to do the kidnapping thrown a wrench into the scheme? Had that person decided he wanted more money? Or had he decided he'd wanted cryptocurrency instead to avoid being tracked? Or was he upset that Parker Hall had allowed himself to be identified, his face plastered all over every news station, locally and nationally?

Any one of those reasons alone or all of them together could have derailed the initial timeline. Although he would've still expected Hall or maybe Hall's replacement to contact them with a new time frame. No matter what they wanted in exchange, they would still need time to pull the funds together in the proper format or to work out a way to gather more funds.

The last thing he wanted to do was ask Bax Scala for more money.

He didn't want to believe he'd been wrong, that this entire nightmare of a scenario might not be about money. Yet if that wasn't the goal, then what was? It didn't make any sense that Caleb had been taken for a different reason.

But as he watched the second hand of the wall-mounted clock tick slowly by, his apprehension grew.

"Brady? Help me understand why this is happening." Grace jumped from her seat to cross over to him. "This is insane. Hall should have called by now."

"I know." He drew her close, ignoring the surprised look Ian flashed their way. "I'm so sorry, Grace. I don't know what to tell you."

"It's bad, Brady," she whispered. "I can feel it."

"Let's pray that Hall has been found and that the police will be contacting us about having him in custody very soon." He honestly didn't believe that to be the case, but he couldn't bring himself to smash her hope to smithereens. "Sometimes these situations take more time than you realize for this to play out. We're going to hear something soon."

"I've been praying, Brady. But it's not working. I can't bear it. Look at the time? It's one o'clock! That's the deadline, Brady. One o'clock!" Grace abruptly buried her face against his chest. He gathered her close, wishing there was a way to ease her pain.

His gaze was glued to the clock. The second hand slowly went around until it was a minute past one o'clock. Then two minutes.

Then five minutes.

Then ten.

Grace's phone remained silent.

CHAPTER TEN

Caleb is dead. Caleb is dead. Caleb is dead!

The words echoed through Grace's mind as panic clawed up her throat, choking her. She couldn't do this. She couldn't go on if her son had been taken from her forever.

Why, Lord, why?

She clung to Brady, her knees going weak. Tears dampened her eyes as she imagined every horrible scenario. The worst was that Caleb had fought back against his abductor, so Parker Hall had hit him too hard, killing him.

Her heart squeezed in her chest. Brady's arms tightened around her, but even that didn't help. Then she realized that Brady had not been given the chance to meet his own son, and that only made her cry harder.

He'd never forgive her for this. And she didn't blame him one bit.

"Don't give up hope, Grace," Brady murmured. "Please don't give up."

In some remote corner of her mind, she heard a door open and close. Keeping her face buried against Brady's chest, she struggled for some semblance of control. Brady was grieving over this too. She swallowed her sobs and tried to stem the flow of tears.

"We're going to find Parker Hall and Caleb," he murmured. "Very soon."

Dead or alive? She was afraid to ask.

She lifted her head from the comfort of his chest and sniffled loudly. "I need a tissue."

"Here." He eased her toward the conference table to grab the box of tissues. She used several to wipe at her face and blow her nose, noting that Ian had left them alone in the room.

Probably because he couldn't stand to watch her melt down.

"He's dead, isn't he?" she asked dully. "That's the only reason Hall wouldn't make the call to set up the exchange."

"I don't believe Caleb is dead, and thinking like that is only going to make this harder than it already is. If Hall was hired by someone else, there are plenty of reasons for a possible delay." Brady's tone was uncharacteristically stern. "We must have hope, Grace. To have faith that God is watching over our son."

She almost said that was a pile of baloney but managed to bite her tongue. He was right about one thing, she couldn't assume Caleb was gone for good. As long as she was alive and breathing, she would continue to search for their son. Pushing her fears aside, she focused on their next steps. "Have you tried calling Parker Hall's disposable phone number recently?"

In response, Brady pulled his phone out and made the call. He put it on speaker so she could hear, but it was no use. Just like the last few times they'd tried, no one answered. "I'm sorry, Grace, but Hall still has his phone off."

"There must be something we can do, other than searching for the car. Or a connection between Parker and the victims of my brother's investment scam." She waved a hand in frustration. "With the FBI and local police officers working the case, we should have him by now!"

"I feel the same way," Brady admitted. "Caleb has been gone too long. This entire case should never have dragged on this long, not when you consider we have a lot of detailed information going out with the Amber Alert."

His comments were not reassuring. "You're the FBI. I need you to find him!"

"I want that, too, Grace. More than ever." Brady suddenly looked exhausted. "We have agents and officers following every lead." His quiet tone brought a fresh wave of guilt.

"I'm sorry." She sighed and leaned against him. "I know this is all my fault. If we lose him . . ."

"We won't." Brady hugged her, pressing a kiss to her temple. "We're in this together, Grace. And I believe we'll find him."

She wished she could say the same, but she couldn't force the words past her tight throat. If Parker Hall was a hired kidnapper, the man paying him could have pulled Hall out and put someone else in charge of Caleb. Another stranger that would be frightening to him.

A stranger that may hurt him.

Wait a minute, there was another possibility. She abruptly lifted her head to look up at Brady. "Do you think Caleb managed to escape?"

Brady's warm brown gaze clung to hers. "I've considered that possibility. You know him the best. Do you think that's something Caleb might try?"

A tiny flicker of hope bloomed in her chest. "Caleb is

smart, and we know he told the kidnapper he wanted to go home and that he used sign language for the word *help*." She frowned as her small kernel of hope evaporated. "But it's been hours. Even if Caleb had gotten away, we would know about it by now. We teach the kids in day care to go to the closest adult or to a police officer for help. The way he used sign language at the fast-food restaurant is proof that he's trying to be rescued." Her shoulders slumped. "Maybe he tried to escape, but the kidnapper caught him and hit him too hard. Caleb could be unconscious, or worse."

"Okay, let's back up a minute. Let's not go down the path of his being injured." Brady looked thoughtful. "We know the license plate was stolen from Greenland Park. If Caleb had chosen that moment to escape, he might still be there."

"Someone would have called the police," she insisted. "There were people in the park, maybe not like the middle of summer, but there were park visitors. I'm convinced Caleb would have run straight to the closest adult for help, the way he was taught."

"You may be right, but I think it's worth heading back there anyway. He could have gotten lost and is still wandering around." Brady gave her another quick hug. "It can't hurt to check it out. And I'll call to ask Matt and Duchess to join us. I have a lot of confidence in Duchess's ability to track Caleb's scent."

The flicker of hope brightened again. Brady was right, they couldn't give up now. "I'd like that."

As they headed toward the door, Brady's phone rang. He showed her the screen so she could see Marc Callahan's name and once again cared enough to put the call on speaker. Her heart thudded painfully against her sternum as she listened to their conversation. "Hey, Marc, I was just going to call you and your brother Matt. We're about to head back to Greenland Park to search for Caleb."

"Coming to Greenland in general is a good idea. I'm heading there now. I take it you haven't gotten a call from Hall regarding a location for the exchange?"

"We have not," Brady said. "And his phone is still off."

"That may be because a patrol officer in Greenland found the black Honda with the stolen license plate on one of the side streets. Unfortunately, the vehicle appears to have been abandoned." Marc paused, then added, "I'm sorry, Brady, the officers spread out to search but have not found Parker Hall or Caleb."

No Caleb or Parker? Grace swallowed hard. Did that mean Caleb tried to escape and Parker went after him on foot? Catching him and hurting him?

"That fits in with our new theory," Brady said quickly as if reading the despair in her eyes. "We think Caleb may have escaped, managing to stay hidden from Hall. It's one reason he may not have called by his own deadline. If Caleb is still in the park, we need Duchess to help find him."

"Okay, I'll check out the black Honda since I'm almost there. The location seems to be relatively close to the park, so your theory is a good one. You should meet Matt and Duchess there. I'll join you as soon as I'm able."

"Thanks, Marc." Brady immediately made the call to Matt. "Are you and Duchess up to searching Greenland Park for Caleb?"

"We did that once," Matt said. "But we are more than willing to search again."

"Please, Matt," Grace interjected. "The kidnapper's Honda was found empty in Greenland not far from the park. The kidnapper didn't call about the exchange, which leads us to believe Caleb escaped and is hiding from him."

"We can be there in less than fifteen minutes." Matt's voice was reassuring. "Duchess is rested and ready to go."

"Bring her vest this time," Brady said. "I want everyone in the park to be on the lookout for Caleb. I don't care if Parker Hall escapes, finding Caleb is our main priority. It's not as if Hall will get too far, especially if he's on foot."

"Understood," Matt agreed. "Meet at the east entrance closer to the restrooms?"

"No, the north entrance," Grace said firmly. "That's where the Cole couple went for lunch. And that's where their license plate was stolen."

"Grace is right, it's important that we start at the north entrance. See you soon." Brady disconnected from the call, quickening his pace to reach the SUV. She eagerly ran around to the other side of the vehicle, finding a spurt of energy she'd thought long gone.

She settled in the passenger seat, hoping and praying that they were going to find Caleb in the park. Maybe God was still listening to their prayers.

Even though she'd given up on Him several times, she tried again, hoping God wouldn't hold her failed faith against her.

Please, Lord Jesus, please guide Caleb to safety!

BRADY FELT A RENEWED surge of energy, feeling as if they were on the right path. He refused to consider the possibility that Caleb was dead.

He couldn't lose the son he'd never had the chance to meet.

"How long until we get there?" Grace was twisting her

fingers again. "Matt and Duchess may already be on Caleb's scent."

"It's only been seven minutes." He was driving as fast as he could through the midday traffic. "I'm sure we'll beat Matt and Duchess there."

"Please hurry." She twisted her fingers harder, so he reached over and took her hand in his.

"We'll find him." Those words had come out of his mouth often over these past thirteen hours, and he wished he could come up with something better, considering they had not yet found the little boy.

He prayed this would not be another dead end.

His phone rang, making him jump. Seeing Marc's name on the screen, he answered. "Did you get more intel?"

"No. The witness who noticed the car did not see a man looking like Parker Hall or a little boy matching Caleb's description." Marc sighed. "Wish I had better news."

Brady silently agreed, but there was no point in saying it. "What about the officers canvassing the area? Someone must have seen them."

"The canvass is coming up empty, too, I'm afraid. But they've only just started," Marc added. "They'll keep going until they hit every house in the neighborhood."

"Thanks, Marc. Matt and Duchess are meeting us at the north entrance of Greenland Park if you want to join us."

"Will do. I like watching Duchess work. If anyone can find a missing child, it's Matt's K-9 partner."

"I know. We'll see you soon." Before he could disconnect from the call, another came in from Rhy. He switched over to answer. "Rhy, I should have told you sooner, but we have not heard from the kidnapper about the exchange."

"I wondered if something had gone wrong. Is there

anything else I can do?" Rhy asked. "Do you expect another ransom demand to come in at a higher dollar figure?"

"I don't know what to think," Brady admitted. "But the Greenland Police found the black Honda with the stolen plates, but there is no sign of Parker Hall or Caleb."

"That's odd," Rhy said.

"Tell me about it. We have Matt Callahan and his K-9, Duchess, coming to search the park as we believe Caleb may have tried to escape. I was tempted to call Quinn to ask if he could go up in the Coast Guard chopper to help search the area, but I doubt he can spot a small child from those heights."

"Maybe with binoculars," Rhy said. "I can ask. You know he'll jump in to help if needed."

"I need everyone in the entire city looking for Caleb." Realizing he sounded depressed and dejected, he quickly added, "No need to run over here, Rhy. I truly think Duchess stands a good chance at finding him."

"We're here for you, Brady," Rhy said. "All you have to do is ask."

He knew that and had already reached out to everyone he knew who could help. "Did you find anything cross-matching Parker Hall's information with Grace's list of day care parents?"

"I dug deep, Brady, but have not found any connection between your perp and Grace's day care kids," Rhy admitted. "I have three more single parents to investigate, maybe something will pop there."

Brady doubted it but simply answered, "Thanks, Rhy. I appreciate everything you've done."

"Call me if anything changes," his brother responded. "I mean it."

"Later." He ended the call and glanced at Grace. "Looks like you were right about your day care families."

"I'm glad Rhy checked them out anyway." Grace looked out the window. "I see the park entrance and Matt's SUV."

He saw them too. He parked directly behind them and joined Matt as he was giving Duchess the scent bag holding Lucy, Caleb's stuffed dog.

"This is Caleb. Seek Caleb!" Duchess stuffed her nose into the bag, then her tail began to wag as she whirled around to play the find-and-seek game. "Seek!"

Duchess lifted her nose to the air, drawing in the myriad of interesting smells swirling around. Brady thought it was nothing short of amazing that Duchess could pick through all the others to identify Caleb's unique scent.

Duchess turned and trotted along the road leading into the park. She wasn't doing the zigzag pattern the way she had before. Nose to the ground, she moved even faster until she abruptly stopped, sniffing intently.

Then she sat and looked up at Matt. This was her alert indicating she'd found the little boy's scent.

"Good girl, Duch." Matt didn't pull out the toy but leaned over to scratch her ears. "Seek Caleb. Seek!"

As if she understood the game wasn't over, Duchess lifted her nose again, then began to move across the field. Brady stood for a moment, estimating this to be close to the location where the Cole couple had left their car to head over to eat their picnic lunch.

The picnic tables were on the other side of the road from where Duchess alerted, making him wonder if Parker Hall had noticed the black car, parked here at the side of the road, then left Caleb to get the license plate. It seemed to be a logical assumption, especially when he turned back in time to see Grace following Matt and Duchess across the grassy lawn heading toward a wooded area off in the distance.

"Brady, it looks like Duchess has Caleb's scent!" Excited anticipation rang through Grace's tone. His own pulse quickened, too, as he watched Duchess lead the way straight into the woods without pause.

He quickly caught up with Grace. Together they watched as Duchess stopped in the wooded area, sniffing the ground intently. Then she moved around a tree and sniffed again. Matt kept an impassive expression on his face, his hands loose at his sides. Brady knew it was important for K-9 cops not to interfere with the dog's scent tracking. Duchess would be eager to please Matt and could give a false alert if she thought he wanted her to find a specific spot.

"Seek Duchess," Matt said again. "Seek Caleb."

Duchess wagged her tail, circled the tree, and sat, staring up intently at Matt.

Brady's breath caught in his throat, watching the dog work. Was this really happening? Had Duchess found a spot where Caleb had hidden from his kidnapper?

Or was that just what Brady wanted to believe?

"Caleb was here," Grace whispered, voicing his thoughts.

"I believe so," he whispered back.

"Good girl, Duchess," Matt praised. Yet he still didn't reach for the toy. He stroked the dog, but then stood back. "Seek Caleb. Seek!"

Brady wondered if the dog would get tired of playing the game but apparently not. She jumped around with seemingly boundless energy, then once again lifted her nose to the wind.

Matt stood off to the side without moving. He simply

waited for Duchess to do her thing.

The K-9 wound her way through the woods, sometimes backtracking in a way that made him wonder if Caleb had done the same thing or if she was having trouble picking up the scent. It bothered him to imagine six-year-old Caleb hiding in the woods and maybe getting lost as he escaped the kidnapper.

He prayed Hall hadn't found him.

Duchess suddenly darted through a small opening between two trees, heading back out into an open area. He and Grace followed through the woods until they too reached the other side.

About twenty yards away, there was a large play area. Exactly the sort of place that would draw a young boy's attention.

"No, that can't be." Grace's hopeful expression fell. "Where are the parents? The families that Caleb would have run to for help? There's no one here, Brady. No one!"

He didn't know what to say because she was right. There weren't any families hanging around who could have stepped forward to save their son from his kidnapper. He struggled to remain calm for her sake. "Don't lose heart, Duchess is on the scent. He may have had to find a family somewhere else."

Grace covered her mouth with her hand as if holding back a scream. He put his arm around her shoulders and guided her forward to the play area. Duchess was sniffing intently around the base of the slide, then she crawled on her belly, sticking her nose into the area beneath the slide. After a long moment, she scooted back out, looked up at Matt and sat.

Another alert? He drew Grace closer to the playground. "Matt? What is Duchess telling us?"

"Good girl, Duch!" Matt took the stuffed animal from his pocket and tossed it into the air. Duchess leaped up to snatch it in her wide jaws, then raced around shaking her head with obvious joy.

"I need to reward her for finds, even if she hasn't found the target," Matt said. "Let's take a look under here." He went down on his hands and knees, peering beneath the slide.

Brady did, too, but couldn't see anything that stood out. But then he frowned and leaned in closer. There was a small bit of fabric stuck to a sharp edge on the underside of the slide.

"Matt, does this look like a piece of a white T-shirt?" he asked.

"Yeah." Matt met his gaze. "Duch crawled underneath before she alerted. It's clear to me Caleb must have been hiding under here."

He nodded and tried not to lose hope. "Maybe he hid long enough to avoid the kidnapper. From here, he may have gone out to find the next closest adult."

"May I see?" Grace asked.

"Sure." He rolled out of the way so she could get down beside him. She stared into the narrow opening, then turned to face him. "I know Duchess found his scent here, but where is he now?"

"We'll have Duchess continue following the scent." He wanted to pull her into his arms but turned toward Matt. "Can she keep searching? Or does she need a break?"

"She's good to go. I usually take breaks at twenty-to-twenty-five-minute increments." Matt turned and called, "Duchess, heel."

On cue, the shepherd spun around and trotted over to Matt. She sat at his side, then daintily dropped the stuffed toy to the ground at his feet. If the situation hadn't been so serious, Brady would have chuckled.

But he didn't have any laughter or joy inside of him the way he used to. Not since this nightmare had started.

Matt picked up the stuffed animal Duchess had returned, then brought out the scent bag again. "This is Caleb." He offered the bag to Duchess, who put her nose in for just a few seconds as if saying, *Yeah, I know who Caleb is.* "Seek! Seek Caleb!"

Duchess jumped up and went to work. Matt gestured for them to get out of the playground area to give the K-9 plenty of room to work.

Brady drew Grace with him as she hadn't seemed to notice Matt's intent. Her gaze didn't leave the dog.

Duchess sniffed around the slide, then trotted toward the swing. She whirled and headed in the direction of the road.

Grace gasped. "What is she doing? Did Parker find Caleb and drag him back to the car?"

"I don't know, let's just be patient and let her work." He didn't like the way the dog was heading toward the road any more than she did.

Duchess stopped at the side of the road, a completely different spot from where she'd originally alerted. Brady estimated the distance between the two locations was about a third of a mile.

The K-9 sat and looked up at Matt, alerting at the side of the road. Brady felt sick knowing this was the end of the line. If someone had driven Caleb away in a car, they were right back to where they'd started.

No, they were worse off. Because they'd found the black Honda. Caleb could be anywhere with anyone.

Even with Parker Hall.

CHAPTER ELEVEN

Caleb had fallen asleep under the slide. A little girl had found him under there, poking at him until he'd woken up. "What are you doing?" she asked.

He'd rubbed his eyes and looked at her. "Resting."

"I take naps in my bed."

Caleb had no idea where his bed was, but now that the girl had found him, he worried the mean man was close by. "Did you see a mean man?"

"No. Did he hurt you?"

"He took me away from my mommy." Caleb wiped his nose on his shirt and crawled out of the small hiding spot, pulling with all his might when the too-big shirt got stuck. "Where is your mommy?"

"At work. I'm with my daddy." The little girl frowned. "Are you lost?"

Caleb nodded. "Yeah, because the mean man took me."

"Okay, let's find my daddy." The little girl stood and walked a few steps away from the play area. He cautiously followed her, looking around to make sure the mean man wasn't standing nearby. "Daddy? Daddy!"

A tall man with light-colored hair came over to meet them. The man seemed surprised to see Caleb. "Libby, did you find a new friend?"

"Yes, he's lost. We need to find his mommy." The little girl skipped over to her daddy. "You'll find her, won't you?"

"Ah, sure." The tall man looked concerned. "Can you tell me your name?"

Caleb rushed toward the girl's daddy, so relieved to have a parent close by. He clutched the man's leg and looked up at him, then said in a formal tone, "My name is Caleb Brady Ramsey."

The tall man smiled and bent to rub a hand over his hair. "Okay, Caleb Brady Ramsey, let's see if we can find your mommy."

Caleb was so happy he cried. "Keep the mean man away from me," he sobbed. "I'm a scared of him."

"Of course, I will. Don't worry, you're safe now." The tall man had picked him up and carried him away from the playground.

———

IT WAS all Grace could do not to crumple into a heap after Duchess had alerted at the side of the road. Losing Caleb's trail had ruthlessly snuffed the flicker of hope burning in her heart.

Caleb was gone, and they had no idea where he was. It seemed impossible that this could be happening. That her son had been missing since midnight and they were no closer to finding him.

They knew all sorts of places he'd been—at the motel where he'd dropped Lucy, at the breakfast fast-food restaurant, the lunch fast-food restaurant, the restrooms at Fall

River Park, and now here at the Greenland Park playground.

But none of that information helped them now.

"Let's get Greenland officers here to help canvass the park," Brady said. "Someone may have seen Caleb leaving the area."

In a car? Highly doubtful but she bit her tongue. Running an investigation was not her area of expertise. And being this close to finding Caleb, only to lose his scent at the side of the road, troubled her.

Horrible scenarios flashed through her mind. Someone else had found Caleb but hadn't notified the police. Or Parker Hall had handed Caleb over to another kidnapper. The abandoned Honda located close by seemed to reinforce that idea.

Caleb must have run away but had gotten caught when he reached the playground. Hall was in trouble with whoever hired him because his name and face was flashed all over the news, so a second kidnapper was brought in to take over. They met at the side of the road, put Caleb in a different vehicle, and then had abandoned the Honda with the stolen plate.

They could be anywhere in any type of vehicle!

Sniffing back sudden tears, she dug for her phone. If that was the way this had played out, she'd get a ransom demand again soon.

Wouldn't she?

"Will do." Matt made a quick call using his radio. She turned away, barely able to stay upright.

Lack of sleep combined with fear and worry were taking a toll. She wasn't sure how much longer she could do this.

Then she mentally kicked herself, hard. Giving up

wasn't an option. She would do this for as long as it took to find Caleb.

"Grace?" Brady's low voice was almost her undoing.

"Someone else has him," she said duly. "Another kidnapper."

"We don't know that." Brady put his arm around her shoulders.

"Don't tell me to have faith!" Her voice was sharp, and she didn't care. She jerked away from him. "That's not what I want to hear. I need to know how you're going to find him!"

"We'll update the Amber Alert." Brady's voice was subdued. "And we'll keep following up on leads as they come in."

It wasn't enough. None of their attempts to find him had been enough! They'd come so close only to have failed each time.

"Brady?" Marc Callahan came over to stand beside them. "I heard Duchess found the boy's scent."

"And lost it at the road." Grace didn't intend to sound ungrateful but couldn't help herself. What little patience she'd managed to hold on to vanished. "Leaving us nothing to use as a clue to help find him."

Brady remained silent, and for some odd reason that only irked her more.

"I'll take Duchess to check the restrooms again," Matt said. "Can't hurt."

"Thanks, Matt," Marc said. He turned toward her. "I know this isn't easy, Grace."

"You don't know!" Her voice rose with anger. "My little boy has been gone more than thirteen hours and is in the hands of a stranger!"

"You have every right to be upset," Brady said.

"Yes, I do." Her spurt of anger abruptly faded. "I just want him home."

Brady's phone rang. After glancing at the screen, he stepped closer to her. "Grace, this is Rhy. Do you want to listen in?"

She managed a nod.

"Rhy, do you have something?"

"I just finished digging into the last of the Grace's day care families. One thing that is strange is that a woman by the name of Angeline Rogers, mother of Taylor Rogers, seems to have sprung out of thin air. It's not just the lack of social media, but I dug into her Social Security number, and it originated out of Texas. I tried to find a Texas driver's license, but that doesn't exist."

Grace frowned. "She's very nice, works at a local restaurant as a waitress. Her son Taylor is well behaved."

"That doesn't mean she isn't hiding something," Brady pointed out. "It sounds to me like she's using a fake Social Security number."

"That's my impression," Rhy agreed. "Could be something as simple as hiding from an abusive ex."

"Or it could be that she has a criminal background she's trying to hide. One that links her to Parker Hall or the man who hired him," Brady said. "Whatever the reason, I'd like to pay this woman a visit."

Grace would never have considered Angeline Rogers to be connected to Caleb's kidnapping. The woman had come across as quiet and shy rather than criminal, but she quickly nodded in agreement. "I'm sure I can get her to confide in me."

Brady grimaced. "This might be a conversation I need to have as a federal agent. Especially if she's involved in this."

Grace bit back a snarl, forcing herself to nod in agreement. "If you think that's best."

Brady opened his mouth as if to say something but must have decided against it.

"I have her address." Rhy recited the information. "She's employed at the Ravenswood Diner."

"Got it," Brady said. "We'll let you know if we come up with anything."

"I'm here for you," Rhy said. "Call anytime."

Despite her anger and fear, Grace was touched by the closeness between the Finnegan siblings. She'd known they stayed connected with frequent phone calls back when she and Brady were dating. And had shared family dinners together. But nothing like this, where his brother had dropped everything to help at a moment's notice.

It shone a bright spotlight on what had been lacking in her relationship with her brother. A man who hadn't cared about how he was harming others when he'd selfishly stolen their life savings. Even her parents had fled to Florida to avoid the scandal of Adam's arrest rather than staying to help her out.

Granted, they'd lost their retirement savings too. They'd sold their Chicago house and taken what equity they'd had to buy a small trailer in Florida. They'd offered to have her and Caleb join them, but the trailer only had two bedrooms, and she hadn't relished the idea of sharing the small living space with them.

What kind of brother steals from his own parents?

None of the Finnegans, that's for sure.

"I'll come with you to interview this woman," Marc said. His gaze darted between her and Brady. "And considering how much you are both emotionally involved in this case, I'll take the lead on questioning her."

There was a long moment as the two FBI agents stared at each other.

"Fine." Brady's tone was curt. "Let's hit the road."

Leaving the last-known location of her son wasn't easy, but Grace turned to follow Brady back to the SUV. This nightmare was beginning to feel like that movie, *Groundhog Day*, where they kept doing the same thing over and over in a loop that never ended.

How many times had they driven from Ravenswood to Greenland to the FBI office and back? Too many to count.

They were only driving for about three minutes when Brady's cell lit up. On the dash console, she saw Matt's name. Had Duchess found Caleb? She tensed as Brady answered the call.

"What's going on, Matt?"

"I just wanted you to know that Duchess picked up Caleb's scent in the men's room," Matt said. "I've asked several people nearby if they saw a man and a boy go inside, and one woman admitted that she noticed a tall blond man carrying a boy inside the restroom. The kid had his arms wrapped around the man's neck and was smiling, so she didn't think it was Caleb."

Grace straightened in her seat. "A tall blond man? Any other distinguishing features?"

"Unfortunately, she didn't pay attention after deciding it wasn't the child on the Amber Alert." Matt sounded frustrated as he sighed. "I grilled her over and over, but she just kept saying the little boy couldn't have been Caleb because he didn't act scared."

Her gut clenched as she imagined what this witness claimed to have seen. "Do you think Caleb was drugged? It would be one way to make him compliant."

"I'm not sure," Matt admitted. "If Duchess hadn't

alerted on Caleb's scent inside the bathroom, I would not have given this woman's statement any credit. But she did, so I have to go on the assumption that Caleb was here with a blond man."

"Thanks for the information, Matt," Brady said.

"I wish we had better news," Matt said. "I'm going to rest Duchess for a while in case you need us again."

"We appreciate that," Brady agreed. "I'm hoping that we'll get another sighting of him soon. We'll be in touch if we learn anything new."

Grace put a hand over her stomach, feeling sick. Caleb had been through so much.

Had her son been drugged? Her gut pitched and rolled. Despite her on-again, off-again relationship with God, she found herself praying that whatever Caleb had been given was something relatively harmless like Benadryl or some other over-the-counter sleeping agent.

And not hard-core street drugs.

———

THE TENSION RADIATING from Grace was killing him. Even worse, it hurt to know she didn't want any emotional support from him.

It was as if the closeness they'd shared over the past thir-teen-plus hours hadn't happened. Giving him the impres-sion she didn't care about him.

The stress of this nightmare was ripping them apart rather than strengthening the bonds they'd once shared. He'd loved her once.

And he'd thought she'd loved him too.

Marc was right to insist on taking over the investigation. Brady had known all along that his colleague would have an easier time remaining objective as they followed leads, even though Marc was a doting father with three kids of his own.

No matter how much Marc might identify with how helpless a parent felt when their child was missing, Caleb wasn't his son.

He was Brady's son.

A son he desperately wanted to find, before it was too late.

When Grace had lashed out in anger, he'd almost responded in kind, reminding her that she'd kept his son from him for six years! Obviously, fighting over the past wasn't helpful. It wouldn't help find Caleb, so he'd used all his willpower to hold back.

The traffic was still light at 1:35 in the afternoon. Hard to believe it was already thirty-five minutes past the original ransom deadline.

No doubt, the blond man who had Caleb would call soon to make new arrangements for the exchange. He hadn't warned Rhy of his concern the new kidnapper would raise the ransom demand. Right now, he didn't want to know if Bax had already reached his limit on accessible funds.

Better to deal with that when they'd gotten the call. He would instruct Grace to push hard to keep the demand the same, emphasizing the fact that getting more would only delay the process.

Grace didn't say anything as he drove. She sat still, not even twisting her fingers the way she had most of the day.

He had no idea what to say to her, so he focused on driving. Staying alert wasn't easy, his lack of sleep had given him a pounding headache. He was sure Grace was feeling the same way.

When they reached Ravenswood, he pulled Angeline

Rogers's address up on his GPS. Conveniently, her apartment wasn't far from the restaurant where she worked.

According to the route on the screen, they would arrive at her residence in five minutes. He called Marc. "Are you close to Rogers's apartment building?"

"Less than five minutes out," Marc confirmed. "Stay in the car and wait for me to call. If she's not at the apartment, we'll swing by the restaurant."

He glanced at Grace. "Sure, you let us know what you find out."

"What is today?" Grace lifted a hand to her head. "Thursday. It's Thursday, right?"

"Yes." He tried to hide his alarm. "Is something wrong?"

"No, I'm trying to remember Taylor's schedule. She brings her son five days a week but often has a day off during the week. I think Wednesdays." She turned to look at him for the first time since they'd gotten in the car. "I'm fairly certain she'll be at the restaurant today."

"Marc will want to check her apartment first anyway." He kept his tone matter-of-fact so as not to upset her. "There could have been a change to her schedule, or her son could have gotten sick."

"I guess." She sounded listless and kept her gaze averted so that she was staring out the passenger-side window. Brady would rather have her get mad and yell at him than sit there like a lump of clay.

But he didn't offer additional encouragement, knowing she wasn't interested in hearing that from him. Not anymore. Having faith and leaning on God during dark days wasn't easy. He remembered that from when his parents had died in the car crash and later when Grace had broken off their relationship.

It was no different today. He needed God's strength and

support now more than ever. And it helped to know the rest of the family was praying for Caleb too.

He found the apartment building and pulled up behind Marc Callahan's SUV, keeping the engine running. He watched as Marc slid out from behind the wheel and headed inside. The building was similar to the one Grace lived in, so he wasn't surprised when Marc was able to walk inside without being buzzed in.

The lax security at her apartment was the least of their problems. He prayed Angeline was inside. Interviewing her at the apartment would be easier and more private than confronting her at the restaurant.

The seconds ticked by with excruciating slowness. When Marc finally reappeared, it was clear from the expression on his face that Angeline wasn't home.

Marc waved in the general direction of the restaurant. Brady nodded and put the gearshift into reverse.

The restaurant wasn't as busy as he'd feared, the lunch hour apparently had dwindled over the past hour. He found a parking spot right next to Marc's SUV. He reached to turn off the engine when his phone rang.

Inwardly groaning at Donovan's name on the screen, he quickly answered. "Hey, boss. Sorry I haven't been in touch to update you on the latest intel we're following up on. Things have been happening fast."

"Where are you?" Donovan demanded.

"Ravenswood, we have a lead on a woman by the name of Angeline Rogers. She uses Ms. Ramsey's day care center; she has a young son who attends each week. From what we've uncovered, she seems to be living under a fake Social Security number. We're at the Ravenswood restaurant where she works. Marc is going to talk to her."

"I have better news," Donovan said. "We just received a

call from the Greenland Police Department. They have Caleb. He was found at the park and brought in by a concerned citizen, a man by the name of Kent Morrison."

"What?" Grace almost screamed. "Caleb's been found? Are you sure?"

"That's the report, but I figured the two of you needed to get there ASAP to verify the boy's identity."

"Thanks, boss. We're heading there now." He threw the SUV into reverse and backed out of the parking spot. Marc lifted a brow in confusion. He lowered the window. "Caleb has been found; he's at the Greenland police station. We're going there now."

A broad smile creased Marc's face. "Great news, Brady. Go and let me know what you learn. I'll stay here to find out what this woman has to say." Marc did a little fist pump. "Gives me hope that humanity isn't too far gone."

"Exactly." Brady found himself smiling back. He lifted the window and squealed out of the parking lot.

"Do you really think the little boy is Caleb?" Grace asked. Her expression was a mixture of fear and hope. "What if they have the wrong child?"

"You gave us a good picture of him to use in the Amber Alert. Besides, I'm sure Caleb has been able to tell them who he is, right? Let's stay positive. I'm thinking the blond guy who was seen carrying him into the restroom may have found him wandering around the park. You said yourself that Caleb would find the closest adult."

"That is what we teach all the kids." Grace reached over to grasp his arm. "I pray he's there, Brady. I've been disappointed so many times over the past few hours, I'm afraid to believe he's been found."

"I know this has been a terrible ordeal, but they wouldn't have called the FBI unless they were certain they had the missing boy." He covered her hand with his. "Try to have faith that we'll see Caleb very soon."

"I will." Her grip on his arm tightened. "Please hurry."

"Trust me, I will." He had to waste precious seconds inputting the address for the Greenland Police Department. Once he knew exactly where they were headed, he drove as fast as he dared, grateful it was too early for the usual rush hour. Not that traffic here was nearly as bad as Chicago. He silently thanked God for watching over his son, deeply overwhelmed with relief that the little boy had been found.

The cop side of him wanted someone to be arrested for this horrible crime. Maybe several someones because he did not believe Hall was acting alone. No one should get away with kidnapping a child. Yet he'd worry about finding Parker Hall later.

The only thing that mattered was reuniting Grace with Caleb.

And seeing his son for the first time.

He held off calling Rhy until they could confirm Caleb's identity. He was glad to know his brother-in-law, Bax Scala, wouldn't need to risk his inheritance on the ransom demand.

The GPS screen indicated they were close. He saw the police station up ahead on the right and swerved into the very first parking space he found. Throwing the gearshift into park, he glanced at Grace. "Ready?"

"Yes." She looked better. Stronger now that the moment was close. Still, she reached for his hand as they headed inside the building.

The first thing Brady noticed was a tall blond man standing beside a young girl and a young boy. His gaze zoomed in on Caleb, instantly recognizing him from the picture Grace had shared what seemed like days ago rather than hours.

"Caleb! Oh, Caleb!" Grace cried.

"Mommy!" Caleb ran straight toward her. He tripped, but Grace was already closing the gap between them. She scooped him into her arms and began to sob.

"Caleb, I'm so glad to see you."

Brady hung back, forcing himself to be content with seeing his son rather than hugging him. His eyes misted, but he quickly brushed the tears away.

"See, Daddy? I knew you'd help him find his mommy," the little girl said.

Brady stepped forward. "I'm FBI Agent Brady Finnegan," he introduced himself. "We want to thank you for bringing Caleb in."

"I'm Kent Morrison." The blond man stepped forward, holding out his hand. As they shook hands, he added, "Oh, you must be Caleb's father."

"I—uh, what makes you say that?" Brady asked in confusion. He knew Caleb looked just like him at that age, but surely a stranger wouldn't have noticed the resemblance.

Kent Morrison chuckled. "I got a kick out of the way your son introduced himself to me as Caleb Brady Ramsey. Including his middle name was cute."

His chest squeezed with a mixture of happiness and profound regret. Despite not telling him about the baby, Grace had given his name to their son.

CHAPTER TWELVE

Thank You, Lord Jesus!

Grace held Caleb close, waves of gratitude and relief washing over her. Caleb clutched her tightly too. She never, ever wanted to let him go. He'd been missing for over thirteen hours, the longest hours of her entire life.

But all too soon Caleb began to fidget. He lifted his head to look at her. "I made a new friend. Her name is Libby. Her daddy helped me get away from the mean man."

"I'm so glad you found a daddy to help you." Grace wiped at her face, hating to think of what Caleb had endured at the hands of the bad man. She turned to look at the blond man, whose name she couldn't remember. "Thank you for bringing Caleb to the police department. I owe you a huge debt of gratitude."

"Hey, I would want someone to do the same for me if something happened to Libby." He frowned as he looked down at his daughter. "I can't imagine what you've been through."

"I pray you never have to experience this," Grace said. Caleb squirmed, so she put him down, even though she couldn't bear to let him go completely. Keeping a hold on his hand, she asked, "Did you find him at the playground?"

"Libby did." The blond man smiled. "He was hiding beneath the slide and must have fallen asleep under there."

"The exact spot where Duchess found his scent." She glanced at Brady. He didn't seem to notice, his gaze was glommed on Caleb. "There was a woman who also saw you taking Caleb into the bathroom. We were afraid you were the kidnapper."

"Yeah, he said he had to go but was afraid to let go of me, so I carried him in." The blond man shook his head. "I checked him over and didn't see any bruises, other than a skinned knee, so I didn't take him to the hospital. He was more frightened of the mean man than anything, but you may want to have him checked by your pediatrician, just in case."

"I will." She crouched down so she was eye level with Caleb. "Does anything hurt? Do you have any ouchies?"

Caleb nodded and pointed to his skinned knee. "I runned away from the mean man and tripped and fell because my shoes are too big."

"You did a good job, Caleb. I'm so proud of you." She bent and kissed the knee, then rose, far too conscious of Brady's intense gaze. "We'll clean that up and get you out of those nasty shoes once we get home."

"Mr. Morrison, we'd like to get a full statement from you, if you don't mind," Brady said. "Once that's on record, you can head home."

"Anything you need," Caleb's rescuer readily agreed. "I hope you get the guy who did this."

"We plan to." Brady turned toward the police officer. "Can we use one of your conference rooms?"

"Sure, this way." The officer led the way.

Grace continued holding Caleb's hand as they followed. A frisson of unease snaked down her spine. She had Caleb, but Parker Hall was still out there. And if he was a hired kidnapper, the way Brady had theorized, the danger was not yet over.

Would they try to strike again?

She told herself Brady and Marc Callahan would find him, both the kidnapper and the person who'd hired him, but her stomach churned with the realization that their nightmare might not be over. In her mind, she didn't understand why on earth Parker Hall or another kidnapper would come after Caleb again, yet how could they know for sure?

They couldn't.

She sat and pulled Caleb into her lap. Letting go of him was not an option, and thankfully, he rested contentedly against her.

He turned his head to look up. "I losted Lucy."

"We found Lucy; a very nice police officer named Matt Callahan has your doggy. We'll get Lucy back from him very soon, okay?"

Caleb relaxed and nodded. She noticed Brady sent a quick text message before turning to face Caleb's rescuer. "Mr. Morrison, I'd like to record this if you don't mind."

"No problem," he agreed. "And you can call me Kent."

Grace listened as Kent reiterated what he'd summarized earlier. His daughter Libby had found Caleb under the slide and had taken him over to meet her daddy.

"I asked him if he was lost, and he said he was," Libby chimed in.

Grace gave her a grateful smile. "You were very brave."

But when Kent repeated how Caleb had identified himself by his full name, Caleb Brady Ramsey and how he was *a scared of the mean man,* she closed her eyes and tried not to cry.

How mean had Parker Hall been?

"You didn't see anyone hanging around as if searching for Caleb?" Brady asked. "Anyone remotely suspicious?"

"No, and I did glance around," Kent said. "To be honest, I had the impression Caleb had been under the slide for a while, maybe even as long as an hour, so I wasn't expecting to see anyone. If so, I'd have called 911 to get an instant police response rather than bringing him in."

Brady nodded and looked thoughtful for a moment. "I can't think of any more questions, but I'll call you if something comes up."

"Fine with me," Kent said. He had his arm around Libby's waist. "Like I said earlier, as a father I can't imagine what you both must have gone through."

"Thanks." Brady gave a nod and shut off the recording app on his phone. "We appreciate everything you've done for Caleb." He turned to address the little girl. "You were wonderful, too, Libby."

The girl beamed. "I helped."

"You sure did." Brady smiled at her, then turned to Grace. "Ready to go?"

"Yes." She was more than ready to go home. Her cramped one-bedroom apartment would be a welcome relief after all of this driving around.

The two men rose and shook hands. Kent and Libby left first. Brady hesitated for a moment, glancing at Caleb as if he wanted to say something. She tensed because this wasn't a good time to spring the news that Brady was his father.

Caleb had been traumatized enough for one day.

Was she taking the coward's way out? She tried to view

the situation logically. She did not want to cause Caleb any more anxiety. As it was, he'd likely suffer nightmares over this.

"I forgot to call and arrange for the bedroom window to be repaired." Brady frowned when they stepped outside. She had Caleb's hand, and he stayed close to her side. "It might be better for you and Caleb to stay with me for a while."

It was on the tip of her tongue to refuse, but just remembering the missing window was enough for her to reluctantly admit that staying in the apartment overnight wasn't an option. Yet she also knew Brady had suggested this arrangement for one main reason.

To spend time with his son. She drew in a deep breath and nodded. "I . . . suppose we can do that."

His jaw clenched as if he were annoyed, but he only said, "Thank you. We'll head back to your place long enough to pack a few bags if that helps."

"Sure." She tried to smile. The moment they'd found Caleb, their relationship had changed. There was an awkwardness between them that hadn't been there before. "Thank you for helping to bring Caleb home."

"I'm glad God sent Libby and Kent to the playground." Brady glanced at Caleb, then back to her. "They are the real heroes of the day."

"You are so right." She silently admitted that God had been watching over their son. To come out of this ordeal with only a scraped knee was nothing short of a miracle. Although she also knew that emotionally it would take Caleb a while to get through this. She made a mental note to call his pediatrician very soon.

She opened the back passenger door for Caleb. "I don't have to sit in a booster seat?" he asked.

Brady frowned. "We can stop and buy one."

"No need, I have one at home in the storage unit. I bought it at a rummage sale in case I was able to afford to buy a car."

His jaw tightened again, and she understood his anger. If she'd told Brady about Caleb, her lack of funds wouldn't be an issue.

"Get inside, Caleb." She gestured for him to climb up. "We'll make do with using the seat belt. This won't be a long ride."

"Okay." He didn't balk at crawling into the car. She buckled the seat belt, tucking the shoulder strap behind him so it wasn't across his face. Then he looked right at Brady. "Who are you?"

"He's a police officer." Grace did not want to have the daddy conversation in the car. "Mr. Finnegan has been looking for you."

Caleb frowned. "How come he doesn't have a policeman uniform?"

"I was supposed to have the day off," Brady answered before she could. "I am a different kind of police officer. I wear a suit not a uniform."

"'Cause you're a boss?" Caleb asked.

"Sort of." Brady must have decided going into more detail would only confuse the boy more. "My brother wears a uniform. You'll get to meet him very soon."

Caleb yawned. "'Kay."

Grace knew the brief nap Caleb had taken beneath the slide probably hadn't provided enough rest for the little boy. She wondered if it would be better to head straight to Brady's without stopping at the apartment, then decided the short detour wouldn't matter. She wanted Caleb to have his own clothes and some of his toys.

Anything to help provide some sense of normalcy after all of this.

Once they were settled in the front seat, Brady backed out of the parking space. He glanced at her. "I texted Rhy but would like to call him too."

"Of course, I understand." The reality of Caleb having eight aunts and uncles was a bit overwhelming. She glanced over her shoulder, then added, "I'd like to wait until later to tell Caleb the truth."

"I'm not going to wait long." Brady's voice was firm. "It's already been six years, Grace."

She winced. "I know. Let's just get settled in first, okay?"

"Okay." Brady made the call to his brother. "Hey, Rhy, just want you to know we have Caleb."

"Thank the Lord," Rhy said. "I'm so relieved to hear it."

"There's no sign of Hall, though, so I want to keep that BOLO out for him."

"Got it," Rhy agreed. "I wish we knew if he was riding a bus, stole a car, or is using a rideshare."

"All are viable options. I would think he'd stick to a rideshare rather than risk being recognized."

"I agree, but we'll keep our eyes peeled." There was a brief pause before Rhy asked, "Don't forget Elly's graduation party a week from Saturday. We'd love to meet Caleb then too."

Grace opened her mouth to protest, but Brady shot her a warning glance. "That sounds awesome. I'm sure Grace and Caleb would love to attend the party."

"Sounds good. Later, bro." Rhy disconnected from the call.

She glanced over her shoulder at Caleb. His eyes were closed as he rested his head against the passenger door.

Hoping he was asleep, she turned toward Brady. "You should have asked me about the party first," she whispered.

"Nope, that's not how this relationship is going to work." He'd kept his voice low, but there was no mistaking the edge of anger. "He's my son, and if I want him to come to my youngest sister's graduation party, then that's what we're doing. You've kept him from me long enough."

She tore her gaze from his, unwilling to admit he was right, at least on the latter point. She had kept Caleb from his father for too long.

But the thought of Caleb being swallowed up within the Finnegan clan brought a hint of panic.

They'd have to figure out a way to navigate this new co-custody arrangement.

There was no going back now.

HIS THANKFULNESS at having Caleb home safe was fading fast. He'd hoped Grace would introduce him to Caleb, telling the little boy he was his father.

She hadn't, claiming it was better to hold off having the conversation later. And then she had the gall to tell him he needed to ask her permission to take his own son to Elly's graduation party!

Yeah, that was so not happening. As soon as they were settled, he intended to set forth a new set of ground rules. One that gave him equal rights and access to Caleb. He would not miss more time with his son. In fact, just the opposite. He deserved to spend as much time as possible with the little boy, establishing the father/son relationship he'd been denied.

The sooner Grace accepted that fact, the better.

He struggled to maintain control. Things would improve once he had Grace and Caleb settled at his place.

Using the hands-free functionality, he called Matt. "Good news, we found Caleb."

"I heard from Marc, congrats." Matt sounded happy.

"I was wondering if we could grab Caleb's stuffed dog, Lucy, from you." He reached up and moved the rearview mirror to better see Caleb's sleeping face. "He's been talking about how he lost it. I think he'll feel better once he has it back."

"Not a problem, I'm currently in Greenland, do you want to swing by? Or I can meet you somewhere."

"Not the park," Grace quickly interjected. "I don't want to bring back any bad memories."

He nodded in agreement. "Tell me where you are, Matt. We'll come to you."

Matt gave the location, which was near a fast-food restaurant that was different from the ones the kidnapper had taken Caleb. Still, he hoped the little boy would sleep long enough for them to get away just in case Grace was right about the nightmares.

Brady turned the SUV around to head in the opposite direction from where they were headed. Maybe he was being ridiculous, but he wanted to give Caleb something that would make him happy.

They drove in silence. When he saw Matt's K-9 SUV, he pulled in alongside him, keeping the engine running. Matt lowered his window and handed the stuffed animal over to Grace.

"I'm really glad the search is over," Matt said. "It's nice to see a great outcome on a case like this."

"You and Duchess helped so much." Grace took the

dog, clasping it to her chest for a long moment. "Thanks for everything."

"Anytime." Matt nodded at Brady. "Good luck with nailing the jerk who did this."

"I'm sure you'll hear when we do. Take care, Matt." Brady raised the windows and backed out of the fast-food parking space. A quick glance at the rearview mirror confirmed Caleb was still asleep. His stomach growled with hunger, but he ignored it. He had food in the fridge and could throw a meal together once they were home.

Home. He had a two-bedroom condo and immediately wondered how long it would take to put it on the market to buy something else.

Something bigger, a house with a nice backyard with a swing set. A place that was child friendly.

Grace reached back to tuck Lucy beside Caleb. The little boy shifted but didn't awaken as he wrapped his arm around the dog, pulling it close.

Brady's throat tightened with emotion. He longed to hold his son in his arms, to protect him from ever being hurt again. He unclenched his fingers from the steering wheel, knowing that hanging on to his anger and resentment wasn't healthy.

Hadn't he told Grace they should move forward, without ruminating over the past? Yeah, it was time to follow his own advice.

"I know you're upset with me," Grace said.

"I'll get over it." He glanced at her. "Having Caleb safe is all that matters. We'll figure the rest out as we go."

"He's been through a lot, Brady. I don't want to overwhelm him."

His being Caleb's father shouldn't be traumatic, but

then again, he couldn't deny the kid had been put through the wringer. "I know. I'll do my best to be patient."

"Thank you."

He nodded and headed toward Grace's apartment building. Reaching Ravenswood didn't take too long, although when he pulled up in front of the building, the place looked even worse in the daylight. It wasn't just Caleb's broken window that bothered him, the entire place looked worn down and not very safe. It hurt to know she and Caleb had been so close all this time, but he held his tongue.

There was a small part of him that admired her for owning and operating a day care center. A logical career for a single mother with a teaching degree.

"I—uh, maybe you should wait here." Grace unbuckled her seatbelt, turning to look back at Caleb. "I don't want to disturb him."

Before he could answer, his phone rang. He quickly turned the volume down, but thankfully, Caleb didn't seem to hear it. "Hey, Marc. Did Angeline Rogers give you any interesting information?"

"Her story is that she moved here from Texas to start over. She says the boy's father is in jail, and I did confirm that. I don't think she's connected to the kidnapping."

"Another dead end," he muttered.

"Yeah. Although I intend to verify her real identity. Her birth name is Olivia Hargrove. Is Grace there? Does that name mean anything to her?"

"No, although I'm not sure I like hearing how she's enrolled her son in my day care under a fake name." Grace frowned, then added, "Marc, will you please let me know if there's something concerning in her past? If she has a criminal record, I don't want to keep her son enrolled in the program."

"I will. Hey, I'm getting a call from our boss, hang on for a minute." Marc switched over to take the call. Brady was about to tell Grace to go ahead and go inside to get her things when Marc came back on the line. "Brady? There's a tip our boss wants us to check out. Someone stumbled across a dead body at Fall River Park."

"A dead body?" Brady sighed. "Why is that our jurisdiction? The local police should be on scene, not federal agents."

"Supposedly the caller thinks the guy looks like the BOLO sketch," Marc explained. "I'll head over, no need for you to come too."

Brady hesitated, then said, "I'd better join you. If this is Hall, we'll need to see if there's any trace evidence linking him to whoever hired him."

Grace latched her seatbelt. "I agree we should go. Caleb is sleeping, so it won't be a problem."

"We're on our way, Marc," Brady said. He pulled away from the apartment building. "Do you have an exact location where they found the body?"

"He was found floating in a pond. Hold on a minute." Marc must have pulled up a map of the area. "Looks like it's on the south side of the park."

"Got it, thanks. We'll meet you there." He ended the call and glanced at Grace. "I'm glad you don't mind riding along. I don't want you staying at that apartment alone."

"I'm not exactly thrilled by that prospect either," she pointed out. "But if the kidnapper is dead, then the danger is over."

"Not if he's been murdered." Brady noticed her wince

and hastily added, "You can stay in the car with Caleb, no need for you to see the body."

"It could be a suicide," she pointed out. "I mean, he did botch the plan, thankfully for us."

"True." He had entertained that possibility too.

She sighed. "It's frustrating that we don't know why this happened in the first place. I mean, we assume it's revenge because of my brother's investment scam, but we don't know that with any degree of certainty."

She was right about that, and the lack of knowledge bothered him. "I'm curious as to why the Honda was abandoned in Greenland, but the body is floating in a pond in Fall River Park."

"He left it there, then tried to drown himself. Or the witness could be wrong about identifying the kidnapper," she said. "As odd as it sounds, I'm hoping it's not him. I would rather he rotted in prison for the rest of his life for taking Caleb from me."

From us, he almost corrected. He cleared his throat. "Witnesses can be wrong, especially under these circumstances." He knew from personal experience with a previous case that dead bodies pulled from the water never looked normal. Mostly because of the bloating and fish bites. Not that he planned to discuss the gory details of waterlogged bodies with Grace. That was the last image she needed to have imprinted in her brain. "We'll find out soon enough."

Ten minutes later, they reached the park. He drove to the south end, stopping abruptly as the road was blocked off by police cars. There were also several news media vans indicating the reporters had shown up. He supposed it was inevitable that they would. Backing up, he found a place to park behind the barricade and away from the news vans. He put the gearshift into park and pushed open his door, before looking back at Grace.

"Why don't you slide in behind the wheel and keep the engine running?" he suggested. "If Caleb wakes up, you can drive around to help lull him back to sleep."

"Okay." She crawled up and over the center console. "How long will you be gone?"

"I'll try to be quick. The crime scene techs might already be here, collecting evidence." He hesitated, wondering if it was wise to leave her, but then he reassured himself there were too many cops around for anything to happen. "See you soon."

She gripped the wheel and nodded. He gently closed the door, then jogged over to where a uniformed officer stood.

He flashed his credentials. "FBI Special Agent Finnegan."

The cop peered at his badge and ID. "Yeah, okay. I heard you guys were coming."

"Thanks." Brady jumped over the crime scene tape and crossed the grassy parkland. The closer he got to the crime scene, the worse it smelled.

Breathing through his mouth, he headed toward a cluster of officers standing around a body stretched out on the ground covered with a black tarp. Off to one side, he noticed two detectives were talking to a young man who was likely the witness who'd called it in.

He held up his creds as he joined the officers. "Agent Finnegan, do you have a positive ID on the body?"

"No wallet, ID, or phone." One of them gestured toward the tarp. "See for yourself."

Brady bent down and peeled the tarp back. The bloated man's face stared up at him. He was missing pieces of skin, but Brady had expected him to look worse. He must not have been in the water for long.

There was no mistaking the resemblance. The dead man looked very much like Parker Hall. They'd have to get dental records to validate his identity as the guy's prints weren't in the system, but he'd bet his last dollar this was the kidnapper.

And the bullet wound in his chest was a good indication he'd been murdered.

CHAPTER THIRTEEN

She couldn't tear her gaze from her sleeping son. Grace was so thankful Caleb was safe and relatively unharmed. The warm sun made her eyelids heavy. Her lack of sleep was catching up with her, big time. Prying her eyes open, she went back to watching Caleb sleep via the rearview mirror.

It made her heart hurt to know he'd need psychiatric help to get through this ordeal. Maybe she'd go with him, if the counselor thought that was a good idea. Anything that would help the little boy get over the trauma of being kidnapped and held for hours. Learning Brady was his father might add a layer of complexity to his treatment needs. She wanted to hold off telling Caleb the news but knew Brady would insist.

Brady. Ironic how she'd been thinking of telling him the truth before Caleb's kidnapping had forced her hand. Had God been nudging her to make the call? She could not deny that Brady's support had been amazing over the past several hours.

Easy to see now how many of Brady's features had been passed along to Caleb. She'd always known he resembled his father, but their shared DNA seemed more prominent now. Especially Caleb's large brown eyes so different from her green.

Her heart squeezed at the thought of Caleb meeting the entire Finnegan family. She met Brady at college and only met them a handful of times before he headed off to Quantico. It wasn't that she didn't think they'd welcome Caleb with open arms, they would. It was more that she had the irrational fear that once Caleb had all his aunts, uncles, and for all she knew, cousins, he wouldn't need her anymore.

Ridiculous for her to worry about that. Caleb would always need his mother. Just like he had a right to get to know his father and their large family.

Caleb made a soft noise but didn't wake up. She caught sight of Brady striding toward her. She scooted up and over the console so he could get in behind the wheel.

The grim expression on his face was not reassuring. She searched his gaze. "The kidnapper?"

"Yeah." Brady glanced back at Caleb, then added, "The ME's office will have to get dental records to make a positive ID, but it looks like Hall. He died of a gunshot wound to the chest, likely murdered by whoever hired him to do the job."

Her stomach knotted. It was difficult to mourn the kidnapper who got what he deserved. But being killed by the man who paid him? That was terrifying in and of itself. "Do you think he'll hire someone else to try again?"

Brady shook his head. "I don't know. Either way, you and Caleb are not staying at the apartment alone. As I said earlier, there's plenty of room at my condo."

She sighed. "That's fine. We don't need to go back to the apartment now. I'd love clothes for Caleb, but maybe it's just safer to stay away."

"I would like to buy him some new things, maybe even a

toy or two." Brady's voice was low. "I'm more than willing to provide for my son."

"I'm not looking for child support," she protested. "I'm not destitute. I'm fortunate that my day care business is doing better this year. Going back to the apartment was more about having items that he knows and is familiar with."

"Needing the money isn't the problem." Brady frowned. "Finnegans don't shirk their responsibilities. If I had known about Caleb, you wouldn't be living in a stupid one-bedroom apartment. Don't you understand? I want to provide for my son."

A headache pounded at her temple from lack of sleep and stress. Arguing with Brady was not helping. "Whatever. Do what you want."

"I will." His jaw was tight again, and she wondered if this was a preview of how their relationship would be moving forward. Brady getting irritated at her provoking a defensive response. The last thing she wanted was for Caleb to pick up on their prickly relationship.

Obviously, they'd have to find some common ground. Some agreement as to how they would co-parent Caleb. She did her best to dial her emotions back.

"I think having new clothes and a couple of new toys would be great for Caleb, thank you."

He shot her a surprised look, then smiled. "Good. There's a store not far from my place. We'll make a brief stop there before heading home." His stomach growled loud enough for her to hear. He flushed, then added, "I'll make an early dinner too."

She glanced back at Caleb. His sleepy eyes were open, and he clutched Lucy close. "I'm hungry."

"He usually has a snack at this time," she explained to

Brady. "Something like crackers to hold him over until dinner. I close the day care at six p.m., so we eat dinner about six thirty or seven."

"Oh, I see." He grinned. "Well, I could use a snack too. A big one. We can get something at the store; they have a snack shop inside."

"That works." She liked the way Brady was willing to adapt his plans for Caleb's sake. In her experience in working with kids for the past six years, keeping a routine schedule was important. "Thanks."

"Of course." She noticed he kept an eye on the rearview mirror and hoped he was looking at Caleb and not for someone following them. The more she thought about the person who'd hired the kidnapper coming after Caleb again, the more her stomach churned. The kidnapper had failed in holding on to Caleb long enough to exchange the boy for the money and had been shot in the chest as a result.

Maybe it was enough to force the guy to get his money back another way. Something less high profile than kidnapping a child.

The streets Brady took reminded her of their frequent trips to the FBI office building. "Are you stopping to talk to your boss?"

"No, my condo isn't far from the office." He shrugged. "When I was first assigned to the Milwaukee office, I stayed closer to the Finnegan homestead. After driving back and forth for two years, I bought a place closer to my job. Rhy and Tarin had the homestead running smoothly by then, so they didn't need my help. And I was closer to Quinn too."

She tried to remember all the Finnegan siblings. "Quinn is a year younger than you, right?"

"Yes. He's with the Great Lakes Coast Guard." He lifted a brow. "Should I quiz you on the others?"

"Please don't. I remember Elly the best, she was very sweet."

"She still is." His smile faded. "She's graduating from her EMT program, which has us all a little worried. Her tender heart is going to take a beating once she hits the streets in an ambulance."

"I'm sure she's tougher than you're giving her credit for. My favorite story is the one where she brought the homeless man in to stay with the family. Only Rhy caught him stealing in the middle of the night."

"Yeah, Rhy gave him cash with strict instructions to never come back or he'd have him arrested." He chuckled. "She's pulled a few crazy rescues, bringing kids, the homeless man, and a variety of pets in over the years. Including a baby coyote that sent Rhy over the edge worse than the homeless guy. He was concerned the pup had rabies, especially after Elly admitted to getting bitten by the thing."

"Oh no! That's terrible!" She glanced back at Caleb, knowing she'd have gone over the edge if something like that happened too. "I bet he was frantic."

"He was, but it turns out the coyote pup wasn't infected. Although that didn't stop Rhy from giving Elly a stern lecture on how painful the rabies shots were. She started crying, which only made Rhy feel worse." He shook his head. "I give Rhy a lot of credit for stepping into the parenting role the way he did after our parents died. He and Elly are still close despite the twelve-year age gap between them. Everyone loves Elly. I just hope she's strong enough to handle the things she'll see while working as an EMT."

"I hope so too." Grace mentally went down the list of his siblings. Alanna was the nurse, that she remembered. "Which one is the firefighter?"

"Colin." He pulled into the parking lot of a large department store. "Let's go. I'll give you the rundown on the siblings later."

She nodded and turned to look at Caleb. "We're going to get you some new clothes and a snack, okay?"

"Okay." Caleb yawned and rubbed his eyes. "I want one of the Avengers too."

"You can pick your favorite," Brady promised before she could answer. "Oh, and I need to buy a booster seat too."

"I have one in my storage area."

He shook his head. "We are not going back to your apartment."

"Fine." She figured there was no point in arguing and tried not to dwell on the custody arrangements they still needed to make.

One step at a time, she told herself. Her life and Caleb's would never be the same. They would be irrevocably changed forever.

Yet even as that thought hit hard, she understood their situation wouldn't be nearly as overwhelming if she took each day one step at a time.

Caleb's mental health and physical well-being were all that mattered. The rest? She'd just have to adapt.

BRADY RAN through the mental list of things he wanted to buy. He had food at his place but probably not the sort of items kids liked. His stomach continued to growl as the three of them went through the store. He started with groceries, learning Caleb liked Eggo waffles, then headed to the children's department for the booster seat and clothes.

Lastly, they hit the toy section. Caleb held two Avengers, one in each hand as if deciding which one he liked better. He was about to buy both but caught Grace's warning gaze.

"One Avenger and one car, that was the deal, remember?" It was the agreement Grace and Caleb had made while they'd picked out groceries. "You already have Iron Man at home, so why don't you pick one of the others?"

Caleb put the Iron Man toy back, keeping Thor. "I am Thor," he said in a low growly voice. "I punch the mean man in the nose."

Grace shot him a look as if unsure of what to say. As if he was the expert? He went with his gut. "You're strong and brave, Caleb, just like Thor." He lightly touched the little boy's arm. "Maybe we can watch the Avengers show when we get to my house."

"Okay. I love it, even though I seen it lots of times," Caleb confided.

"Now you can choose a car, then we need to check out." Grace looked wryly at the full cart. "That will take a while."

"Then Mr. Brady says we can have a snack?" Caleb asked.

"Yes, that's right," Brady agreed. He wasn't keen on being referred to as Mr. Brady, the way Grace insisted, but the middle of the store wasn't the place to have a conversation about calling him daddy.

But soon. He longed for Caleb to know he was his father.

"Goody." Caleb ran over to the car section, peering at the selections with the same intensity he had when looking at the various Avengers action figures. Included in the clothing items was a new pair of Avengers pajamas, this time in red rather than blue.

Almost twenty minutes later, and putting a sizable dent in his wallet, they were seated in a booth in the small café.

Since they'd spent more time than she'd anticipated, Grace indicated they should basically order dinner, forgoing the snack idea.

Brady ordered burgers for himself and Grace, along with a hot dog for Caleb.

"Let's say grace," Brady said.

Caleb looked at his mom in confusion. "Mr. Brady means we should say a prayer," she clarified.

"How come?" Caleb asked.

"Because we need to thank God for our blessings." Brady took the little boy's hand. "Dear Lord, we thank You for keeping Caleb safe in Your care. We are also grateful for the food we are about to eat. Amen."

"Amen," Grace murmured.

Caleb didn't say anything but tugged his hand away so he could pick up his hot dog. "Yum."

"Glad you like it." Brady hid his disappointment over Caleb's lack of familiarity with faith and prayer. Once the boy spent more time with the Finnegans at the homestead at family meals, he'd catch on. The entire family had grown up with faith and attending church, an example set by their parents before their death.

A practice Rhy had embraced after he'd taken over as head of the family.

Brady decided there was plenty of time to teach Caleb what he needed to know. For now, he cherished these moments they were together. Even something as ordinary as sharing a meal was incredible.

Caleb dripped a dollop of ketchup onto his dirty shirt. Grace reached over with a napkin to dab at it. "We'll need to give you a bath when we get to Mr. Brady's house."

The little boy wrinkled his nose. "Do I have'ta?"

"Yes." Grace was firm. "Afterward, you can change into your new pajamas."

"Why did the mean man take my old ones?" Caleb asked. Brady's heart squeezed at the innocent question. Before he could think of a response, Caleb continued. "He said we were playing hide-and-seek, but I didn't believe him."

"I'm sorry the mean man took your pajamas," Brady said. "But he's gone now, so you don't have to worry about him anymore."

"Did you put him in jail?" Caleb's brown eyes still held a hint of fear. "Will he be locked up forever?"

Brady didn't like lying, but in this case, he decided it was justified. For Caleb's sake. "Yes, the mean man is locked up in jail forever."

"Good." Caleb leaned forward to sip from his chocolate milk.

Overall, Brady thought the little boy was dealing with his ordeal pretty well. There would be nightmares, of that he had no doubt. But maybe the way Caleb had run away, effectively rescuing himself, had given him the strength he needed to put it aside.

He knew the FBI psychologist they had on staff would want to question Caleb at some point. Even though Parker Hall was dead, she would want to understand what information Caleb had retained from the incident. And maybe how badly he'd been scarred by the ordeal.

Something he'd need to discuss with Grace very soon.

They finished their meal and took their cart full of items out to his SUV. Out of habit, he glanced around but thankfully didn't see anything alarming.

He quickly secured the booster seat. He bent to pick up

Caleb, but the little boy pushed his hand away. "I wanna do it by myself."

"Okay." He stood back so Caleb could climb in. Then he double-checked the seat belt to make sure it was fastened correctly, before heading around back where Grace was storing their groceries and other items.

"He can be stubborn," she said in a low voice.

"Just like his mom," Brady responded.

"Yeah, like the Finnegans don't carry that gene in their DNA," she scoffed.

Brady couldn't deny it. That stubborn streak had gotten him through Quantico and had prevented him from seeking Grace out afterward. He finished storing the bags, then stepped back to close the hatch. "I hope we can talk to him tonight, after his bath."

"I think it's better if we wait until tomorrow." Grace avoided his gaze. "He's been through a lot, Brady. I don't want to hit him with too much at once."

He bit back a flash of anger. "I hardly think telling him I'm his father is akin to being kidnapped by a mean man."

She flushed. "No, but he'll have a lot of questions that we won't be able to answer."

"I can answer them," he shot back. "He's going to be part of the Finnegan family, end of story."

"It's not that easy, Brady, and you know it." Her gaze narrowed, a steely look flashing in her eyes. "Not tonight. We'll discuss our options after Caleb is sleeping."

He wanted to push back but forced himself to nod in agreement. Mostly because he didn't know how Caleb would react to the news. He'd hoped the little boy would be happy to have a dad.

But Grace's concern gave him pause.

He pushed the empty cart into the rack before sliding in

behind the wheel. He noticed Grace had taken the car from the box and had given it to Caleb.

"Vroom." He slid the car up the rear passenger door and over the windows. He winced a bit at the scraping sound on the glass, then silently chided himself for caring about something so minor as scratched windows. He'd take that and more without complaint.

He'd nearly lost the son he hadn't known about. There was nothing more important than the little boy's happiness. Especially if playing with cars, Avengers action figures, and his Lucy dog helped keep the nightmares away.

His phone rang as they headed toward his condo. Seeing Marc's name, he answered without hesitation. "Hey, Marc. I should have mentioned I'm heading home with Grace and Caleb."

"Glad to hear it. I—uh, thought you should know the FBI team in Chicago put a set of fingerprints they took from Hall's house into the AFIS system. They're a match to our DB."

"Thanks for the information." Brady appreciated how Marc had very carefully used the DB for *dead body* knowing that both Grace and Caleb were listening in. "I figured as much, but it's good to have solid confirmation."

"I'm working a few angles but need to head home too," Marc said. "Kari and the kids are waiting for me. I'll call when we can talk more freely."

"Sounds good. Thanks again for everything." Brady owed his colleague a huge debt of gratitude.

"Later." Marc ended the call.

"So it was him," Grace said in a low voice.

He nodded but kept an eye on Caleb, who thankfully hadn't paid much attention to the adult conversation. "I'll need to conference with Marc at some point."

"I know." She rubbed her temple. "I thought I'd feel better by now."

"You and Caleb will be safe with me." He considered asking for time off work to help Grace and Caleb through the next few days. He was looking forward to bringing her and Caleb to the Finnegan homestead that weekend for Elly's graduation party.

She nodded but didn't say anything more. Brady decided he'd give her tonight to recuperate and to make sure Caleb was okay, too, but he would not wait much longer. First thing tomorrow morning, he would insist on telling Caleb the truth about how he was his father.

He pulled up in front of his condo and hit the garage door opener. He drove inside but didn't close the door right away. The space was small, and he would need room to get their groceries and clothing items out of the back and into the house.

"Take Caleb inside," he suggested. "I'll grab this stuff. Make yourself comfortable in the guest room, there are extra toiletries in the closet."

"Okay." She hesitated, then asked, "You live alone?"

"Yes." He frowned. "I would tell you if I was involved with someone, Grace. I'm not."

She nodded and took Caleb's hand to go inside. Before they could take a single step, he heard a female voice.

"FBI Agent Brady Finnegan?" A woman holding a microphone labeled with a popular news station seemed to come out of nowhere. "How does it feel to know you've helped to find your son?"

"What?" He stared at her in horror, then snapped, "Stop right there. You don't know what you're talking about."

"I do know what I'm talking about." There was a smug

look on her face. It took a minute for him to place her face with the news station she worked for. Her name was Desiree Marks, and he couldn't help but wonder where in the world she was getting her information.

Her all too accurate information.

Desiree turned to look at Grace. "Ms. Ramsey, do you have anything to add? How does it feel to know that the father of your son was instrumental in getting him back from the kidnapper?"

"She has no comment! Take Caleb inside, I'll be in shortly." Brady took a step forward, putting himself between Grace and this nosy reporter. "I have no comment, Ms. Marks, and you're trespassing. I'll give you exactly thirty seconds to get off my property, or I'll arrest you myself."

"I'll leave as soon as you give me an update. Our viewers deserve to know if there is a threat to other children." This woman had the tenacity of a bulldog, which only annoyed him more. "You owe it to them to put their minds at ease."

He didn't owe her viewers squat but managed to control his temper with an effort. "There is no threat to any children. That is the end of my statement. Do not publish anything else, understand?"

"The information on the child being yours is already out there," Desiree Marks said. "I'm just here to confirm our source."

"No comment." Brady put the bags back in the car and reached for his badge, flashing it in her face. Behind her, seeing a camera man videotaping the entire fiasco made his blood boil. "Leave! Now!"

Desiree stared at him for a long moment before turning away. He wrestled with his temper for another moment before understanding dawned.

They couldn't stay here. Not after this. He had no doubt Desiree would blast the thirty seconds of their exchange on the news. If the mastermind behind the kidnapping was watching their local news, he'd know exactly where they were staying.

Stepping back, he slammed the hatch with more strength than needed. He hurried inside the house where Grace and Caleb were hovering in the kitchen.

"Sorry, we need to get back in the car." He held the door between the garage and the house open for them. "We're leaving right now."

"And going where?" Grace asked.

"The Finnegan homestead," he answered without thinking it through. "At least for tonight. We can find another place to stay tomorrow if needed."

She looked as if she was about to argue, so he raised his hand. "We can't stay, Grace. Not after this."

"Fine." She knelt beside Caleb. "We need to go for another ride, okay?"

"I don't wanna," Caleb protested. Brady understood, the kid had basically been stuck in a car most of the day.

"I know, but it's a short ride this time, I promise." Grace urged him toward the door. Her accusing gaze met his. As if he'd leaked the information about being Caleb's biological father.

He hadn't, but he wished he knew who was responsible. Not just for blasting the news to the world, but for putting his son's life in danger all over again.

CHAPTER FOURTEEN

How had the reporters uncovered the truth about Caleb's paternity? The question swirled through her mind as she helped Caleb get back into his booster seat. He squirmed, trying to get out, but she held him in place and quickly fastened the seat belt.

"Noo," he fussed.

"Please, Caleb, it's only a short ride."

"I'm sick of riding in the car." His lower lip trembled, making her feel awful. But she agreed with Brady, they couldn't stay here. Not if the media had found them.

"Let's sing songs!" She began to sing. "The wheels on the bus go round and round."

To her surprise, Brady joined in too. As he backed the SUV out of his condo garage, closing the door behind him, they were all three singing together. Her voice faltered when she saw the news van and the same reporter standing at the end of the street. It appeared the woman was doing a live report.

On Caleb.

She glanced at Brady's grim profile, understanding he wasn't any happier about this turn of events than she was. Maybe he hadn't leaked the information, but then, who had? She and Brady were the only ones who knew.

Wait a minute. So did the good Samaritan who'd rescued Caleb in the park. What was his name? Kent Morrison.

Kent must have been the source of the leak. And really, she couldn't blame the guy, there's no way he could have known to keep the news a secret. Besides, she was the one who'd given their son the middle name of Brady.

She continued singing, hoping to distract Caleb. Or maybe to keep herself preoccupied. Brady sang, too, but his gaze darted everywhere—right, left, to the rearview mirror, then back to the road. A chill snaked down her spine as she realized he was searching for the man who'd masterminded the kidnapping.

Brady broke off singing. "I need to make a quick call. Rhy needs to know we're on our way."

"Caleb, let's take a break." She twisted in her seat to look at him. "You have Lucy, Thor and your car, right?"

"Here." Caleb held them all up for her to see.

"Good, just play for a few minutes, then." She turned back to face forward.

"Rhy? It's Brady. We're on our way over and need to stay the night."

"All three of you?" Rhy asked.

"Yes." Brady hesitated, then added, "If there isn't enough room, we can head to the American Lodge motel."

"No need, there's plenty of room," Rhy assured him. "Tarin and Joy have their own place, and Alanna has moved out too. We only have Aiden and Elly; there are still plenty of bedrooms. You want to give me a hint as to what's going on?"

"I'll fill you in later. See you in fifteen to twenty minutes."

"The whole family knows, don't they?" she asked in a low voice.

"Yes." He shrugged. "To be honest, Rhy recognized the resemblance between me and Caleb when he saw the Amber Alert. I'm sure he told the rest about Caleb by now." He shot her an arched look. "The Finnegan family sticks together no matter what."

She looked away, sensing the hidden meaning in his words. The way she'd kept Caleb a secret was the exact opposite of the family sticking together.

Thankfully, the trip to Brookland didn't take too long. When Brady pulled up in front of the Finnegan homestead, as they referred to it, a wave of apprehension washed over her.

She had not seen Brady's family in a very long time. Several months before the night they'd spent together prior to his leaving for Quantico.

She didn't think they would be mean or nasty, that wasn't their way. But angry and upset at her for keeping Caleb a secret? Yeah, no question about that.

Brady parked in the wide driveway in front of a three-car garage. The redbrick house was larger than she remembered. Or maybe it was just that her apartment had been so small that everything else seemed grandiose. He pushed out of the car, then came around to their side. "Ready?"

Not even close, she thought wearily. But she didn't say anything. With a nod, she climbed out of the car while Brady unbuckled Caleb from his booster seat. The little boy didn't seem to mind, he was happy enough to be out of the car.

"Do you live here?" Caleb asked.

"No, but my brothers and sisters live here." Brady smiled. "You'll like my family, Caleb. They're all wonderful."

Caleb hung back, looking up at her. She hastened to reassure him. "This will be a nice place for us to stay, Caleb. Let's take our things inside, shall we? Don't forget, you need to take a bath."

Brady opened the back hatch and pulled out several bags. She took whatever was left and followed him inside.

Of course, Rhy was sitting at the kitchen table, waiting for them. A pretty woman with long dark hair was beside him. They were huddled close, and when she saw their wedding rings, she realized they were married.

"Hey, Brady," Rhy drawled. His eyes zeroed in on her, then dropped to Caleb. "It's good to see you."

"Rhy, Devon." Brady set the bags of groceries on the counter. "This is Grace Ramsey and Caleb. Grace, you remember Rhy. Devon is his wife."

"Nice to meet you." She set her bags down too. Caleb hung close, as if unsure of the strangers in the room. "Caleb, say hi to Mr. Rhy and Ms. Devon."

"Hi," he mumbled, then hid his face against her.

The long look Rhy exchanged with Brady indicated they'd expected to be introduced as Uncle Rhy and Aunt Devon. She squashed a flash of guilt. This had been a long day for Caleb. He needed to feel safe and secure rather than being told about another life-changing event.

"Caleb is feeling shy. I'd like to get him cleaned up and changed into his pajamas," she continued, ignoring the pointed looks between the Finnegan siblings. "Do you mind showing me to our room?"

Before Brady could answer, Elly came into the room. "Grace! Oh, and this must be our nephew, Caleb." Elly beamed with enthusiasm. "I'm so happy to meet you."

"Hi, Elly." Grace looked past the youngest Finnegan, half expecting to see Aiden behind her. "I was just explaining that Caleb is feeling shy and has had a long day. I'd like to give him a bath and get him changed."

"Sure thing. I just finished sprucing up the bedrooms." Elly glanced at Brady. "I can take Grace and Caleb up if you'd like."

"Thanks, Elly." Brady was putting the groceries away. "I'll bring up the rest of the items from the store shortly."

"Thanks." Grace nodded at Devon and Rhy. "We appreciate you allowing us to stay."

"Anytime," Rhy said. "You and Caleb are always welcome."

She wasn't sure what to make of that comment, so she simply smiled and turned away. "Come, Caleb. Let's go see our rooms."

Elly led the way upstairs. "It's so great to meet Caleb. I love the idea of having young kids playing here." She went down the hall and opened the door to one bedroom, then the one right next to it. "You and Caleb can use these rooms next to mine. Rhy and Devon are in the master suite, and Aiden is in the room at the other end of the hall."

"What about Brady?" she asked.

"Oh, there are six bedrooms, so he can use the guest room," Elly assured her. "I'm giving you Alanna's old room. These rooms have been empty for a while now since Tarin and Joy got married and bought a place of their own, and Alanna moved out."

"What about the others? Quinn and Colin?"

"They haven't been here for a few years. Quinn in particular is off with the Coast Guard for extensive periods of time. Aiden gets deployed often, too, but he hasn't bothered to move out yet. Colin got a place closer to the fire department where he works." Elly paused, then added, "You should know we're really happy to hear about Caleb."

Grace flushed. "You're not angry?"

Elly hesitated and shrugged. "I won't lie to you, Grace. We all were a bit angry at first. Only because we missed the fun baby years. But honestly, we're thrilled to have the chance to know Caleb now." She turned and gestured to the bathroom. "Feel free to use whatever you need in here." Elly dropped to her knees beside the little boy. "Caleb, I hope you enjoy your bath."

"Thank you." Grace thought if she had to keep smiling, her face would crack into thousands of pieces. This wasn't at all how she imagined introducing Caleb to the Finnegans. And their warm welcome only confirmed her deepest fear.

That Caleb would be swallowed up into the Finnegan family, leaving her standing on the outside, looking in.

"HEY, HOW ARE YOU HOLDING UP?" Rhy asked, his gaze full of concern.

He'd brought in the rest of the items from the SUV and had moved vehicles around so that he could park in the garage, hiding it from the prying eyes of the reporters. He turned to face his brother, leaning against the kitchen counter. "This has been the best day and the worst day of my life."

"A shock in more ways than one," Rhy drawled. "I gave the siblings the forgiveness lecture, so don't worry about Grace. They won't say anything bad to her."

"I said more than enough," Brady admitted. "I'm glad she came to me when she needed help, but if the kidnapping hadn't happened? I would probably still be clueless about Caleb. And that makes me really mad and glad at the same time."

"Let's focus on the glad part, okay?" Rhy grinned. "At least we know the Finnegan name will continue on. I'm sure our parents are up in heaven beaming with pride as we speak."

He chuckled. "If you only knew how many times I thought of them today. Despite everything, I'm sure they would have welcomed Caleb with open arms too."

"Of course they would, after giving you a lecture about being irresponsible." Rhy's grin faded as he tipped his head. "Seriously, Brady, it's wonderful you found Caleb, but what I really want to know is what made you decide to come here tonight?"

"A news reporter showed up at my condo." He dropped into a chair across from Rhy and Devon. "Somehow they learned that I'm Caleb's father."

Rhy let out a low whistle. "How did that intel get out?"

He waved a hand. "Possibly the rescuer, Kent Morrison, spilled the beans. But that part doesn't matter. After that reporter Desiree Marks showed up at my condo, I didn't dare stick around. Not when we still have no idea who is behind the kidnapping."

"I thought Parker Hall was the kidnapper?" Devon asked.

"Yeah, but he's been murdered. The police pulled his body out of the pond at Fall River Park with a gunshot wound to the chest. My theory is that whoever hired him got rid of him for messing up the kidnapping plan." Brady sighed. "We're pretty much back to square one in the investigation."

"Not good," Rhy said. "I'm glad you came; we'll keep Caleb safe with us."

"I feel guilty for bringing danger to the homestead. But I had to get out of there, and Caleb was getting antsy." He held Rhy's gaze. "My offer to head over to the American Lodge is still open."

"No, you should stay," Devon said. "Right, Rhy? You brought me here back in January, and keeping a little boy safe is even more important."

"I'm not arguing, Devon. They should stay, but keep in mind, it's not as if the Finnegan name isn't well known in Brookland." Rhy spread his hands. "I hate to point out that the reporters can find you here just as easily."

"I know, but I feel better knowing there're more people around here." Brady rubbed the back of his neck. "I'm at the point where I'm not seeing clearly, my lack of sleep is catching up to me. I'd like to stay here for tonight. We can move on tomorrow if needed."

"You're welcome to stay as long as you need." Rhy glanced at Devon. "We will do whatever is necessary to protect Caleb."

Brady had known the Finnegans would band together for his son. "Thanks." He stood. "I need to get this stuff upstairs for Grace. We also need to have a little heart-to-heart about our son."

"Don't go after her like a bulldozer," Rhy advised. "Keep in mind, you'll need to work with Grace for the rest of your life. Stay focused on what's best for Caleb, okay?"

"Yeah, I hear you." Hadn't he given himself the same

lecture? "I think part of the problem is that Grace seems to think Caleb will be stressed out to learn the truth."

Rhy winced. "I can see how that hurts, but she knows Caleb better than anyone else. You both want the same thing for your son."

"We do." He picked up the bag of clothes. "Thanks, Rhy. I appreciate the advice." Brady walked up the large, curved staircase leading to the second floor. He noticed one of the bathroom doors was closed. He leaned close to listen and could hear Caleb splashing away in the tub.

"Grace?" He rapped lightly on the door. "I have the new clothes here."

"Uh, okay. Just leave them there. I'll grab them in a minute."

He was irritated that she hadn't invited him to join them but did as she asked. He found the guest room and stood for a moment, remembering how he'd had to share a room with Quinn when they were growing up.

It made him think about his future with Grace. He cared about her very much. If he were honest, he'd admit he'd had trouble getting over her. Seven years had passed, yet the hole in his heart had made him shy away from commitments.

She was also very different from the carefree college girl he'd fallen in love with. And he had to assume it wasn't just having Caleb that had given her an added layer of maturity but the responsibility of discovering her brother's fraudulent activities and then turning him and the evidence over to the feds.

He never would have sacrificed his son to stay in the Quantico training program, but he could see how Grace had thought that breaking things off with him was a way to protect his career. If they had continued seeing each other and had gotten married when he was finished with his training, the way he'd hoped, having a brother-in-law who was a convicted felon at the federal level would have been a problem.

And underneath all of this was the fact that he should have followed up with Grace in person rather than taking her word for it. Especially considering their intimacy. He needed to own his role in this.

Since he hadn't taken the time to pack anything from his condo, he turned and headed back into the hall. He ducked into Aiden's room to borrow some of his brother's things. When he stepped out of his youngest brother's room, he stopped when he saw Grace and Caleb emerge from the bathroom. The scent of baby shampoo wafted toward him. Caleb's hair was damp, his cheeks rosy, and he proudly wore his new red Avengers pajamas.

"Hi." Grace smiled awkwardly. "I know it's only seven thirty, but I was just getting ready to read Caleb a bedtime story."

Personally, he was amazed Caleb had managed to stay awake this long. "Can I listen in? Did we buy books that I don't remember?"

"Ah, of course you can join us." She looked flustered at the prospect. "No, we didn't buy any books, but I've read several that I know by heart."

He nodded. "Great, I can't wait to hear them."

"This way, Caleb." She ushered him toward the room next to the one Alanna used to have. "See? Lucy is already in bed ready to snuggle."

Caleb glanced up at him curiously before climbing up. He jumped on Lucy the stuffed dog and rolled around with her.

"Get under the covers," Grace said. "Hurry up now."

Brady sat on the edge of the bed as Grace and Caleb sat with their backs against the headboard. He wished he could hold Caleb, too, but he was content to watch them for now. Grace told the story of *Goodnight Moon*. Caleb's eyelids drifted closed before she finished.

She switched off the lamp, plunging the room into darkness except for the dim beam from the hallway light. Brady rose and followed her out.

"I know you're as exhausted as I am, but I'd like a few minutes of your time."

Elly came up the stairs, beaming at them. "Hi, guys."

"Alone," he added, scowling at his sister. "Let's walk outside."

Grace sighed. "Okay, fine. But I am really tired, and I don't want to be away from Caleb for too long in case he has a nightmare."

"I understand." He glanced at his sister. "Keep an ear out for Caleb, will you? We'll be back in fifteen minutes."

"Take your time." Elly waved a hand. "I'll keep my door open so that I can hear him if he wakes up."

He sensed Grace's hesitation, but she turned to head back down to the main level. Rhy and Devon were in the living room as he'd expected, so he led the way outside.

The spring air was cooler now but still nice. He turned to go into the backyard, where they could have a modicum of privacy. The neighborhood was safe. He had fond memories of playing in Brookland when they were young, biking and playing various games with the neighbor kids.

It was the type of life he'd hoped to pass down to his kids. Funny how things rarely turned out as planned.

"I know you want to tell Caleb that you're his father, and I think we can do that tomorrow after breakfast." Grace glanced over at him as they headed to the center of the backyard. "I assume you're not going to work in the morning?"

"I was hoping to work the case from here. Marc and I are going to touch base in the morning."

"Okay, so that should work out well, then. After breakfast," she repeated, as if needing to convince herself. "I want to give Caleb plenty of time to get accustomed to the idea."

"Grace, I'm not sure why you think he'll be upset about this." Brady felt a bit defensive. "It's not like my family has a criminal background." As soon as the statement left his mouth, he wanted to pull it back.

"Like mine, you mean? Gee, thanks."

"That's not what I meant." He blew out a breath. "I just meant we're a close-knit family of faith. Good role models all the way."

"I know that. It's just . . ." Her voice trailed off. After a long pause, she added, "I don't want you to take him away from me."

He abruptly stopped, tugging on her arm so she was facing him. "I would never do that, Grace. You're Caleb's mother. Nothing could ever change that."

"You and your family could fight for custody and win," she whispered.

Tears glittered in her eyes, making him realize how much she'd tortured herself with this possibility. No wonder she'd been putting this conversation off. "Not happening, Grace. I thought you knew me better than to think I'd do something like that. I thought you loved me."

"I did, but that was a long time ago." Her words were like a knife to his heart.

"I've never loved anyone else, Grace. Not the way I loved you." He pulled her close. "Stop making up bad scenarios in your mind. Caleb is our son. We will raise him together."

"Oh, Brady. I don't deserve your kindness." She knocked him off balance when she went up on her tiptoes to kiss his cheek.

He turned just enough to capture her mouth with his, the way he'd longed to do since their earlier kiss. Grace melted against him, returning his kiss with enthusiasm. Crushing her close, he was astounded to realize the passion they'd once shared had so easily reignited all these years later.

As if they'd never been apart.

After a few minutes, he broke off the kiss. "Ah, Grace, I've never felt like this with anyone else."

"Me either." She lifted her head to look up at him. "I thought I was being so noble breaking things off, but all I've done is made us both miserable."

No argument there, he thought. A dark shadow emerged from behind the large maple tree. Brady reacted quickly, pushing Grace behind him to face the threat. He reached for his gun.

"Don't bother with that," a male voice drawled. "I'm armed. Keep your hands where I can see them."

"Neal? What are you doing here?" Grace asked.

It took a moment for him to remember Neal was the guy she'd dated and remained friends with. Brady froze; the reflection of the streetlight bounced off the gun in Neal's hand.

"You didn't realize it was me, huh?" Neal's smile was evil. "I figured you had since I knew about your baby. And that Brady was his father."

"Why would you do this? Why terrorize a six-year-old child?" Grace's voice rose with agitation. "You didn't love me, and you certainly didn't want Caleb. Why would you pay Parker Hall to kidnap him?"

"You're so stupid," Neal hissed. "Didn't you realize my mother lost her entire retirement fund to your brother's investment scam? That was your fault, Grace. If you and I hadn't been seeing each other, she never would have invested with your crooked brother. It's well past time you pay my mother back."

"I had no idea your mother invested with Adam," Grace cried. "I never told her to do that. I'm not responsible for what Adam did."

"Ah, but you are," Neal countered. "And since Parker blew it with Caleb, I guess you'll have to be the one I hold for ransom. I'm sure the feds will pay to rescue you too."

"That's not happening," Brady said flatly. "You may as well turn around and leave while you still can."

"Grace, come with me right now," Neal repeated. "Or I'll shoot Brady to get him out of the way."

"He's bluffing, Grace, don't move." Brady didn't dare take his gaze off Grace's former boyfriend, trying to find a good moment to jump toward the guy to disarm him.

"Don't, please, don't shoot anyone," Grace begged. She stepped out from behind him with her hands outstretched. "I'll go with you, Neal. I'll be your hostage. No one else has to get hurt."

"If you do as I say, no one will," Neal said.

"He's lying, Grace. As soon as he has you, there's no reason not to shoot me. Isn't that right, Neal?" Brady took a small step forward, wishing desperately Grace would move out of his way. "I'm sure you realized just how close we were to finding the connection between you and Parker Hall."

"He was my idiot cousin, so yeah, I knew you'd make

the connection sooner or later." Neal scowled. "Come closer, Grace. We're leaving right now."

"Get down!" The shout came from behind him. Brady instantly lunged toward Grace, knocking her to the ground just as the report of gunfire reverberated through the night.

CHAPTER FIFTEEN

Grace hit the ground hard beneath Brady's weight, her chin sinking into a muddy patch of grass. She was inwardly reeling over the news that Neal Josling was the mastermind behind the kidnapping.

He'd never told her his mother had invested money with Adam. If he had, she would have shoved him to the top of her suspect list. And she vaguely remembered now that Neal had mentioned his cousin Parker.

"Got him," a male voice called out. Because of Brady covering her, she couldn't lift her head to see who was out there.

"Thanks, Rhy." Brady's voice was muffled. He rolled off and struggled to his feet.

Pressing her hands to the grassy earth, she pushed herself to her hands and knees. Then she glanced over to where Neal was lying on the ground. Rhy kicked the gun out of reach, then knelt beside him. "He's still alive, call 911."

"On it," Brady said.

She stared at Neal for a long moment. Any kindness

she'd once felt for him vanished. He'd done this. He'd kidnapped Caleb! And he'd been about to kidnap her too.

She sat back on her heels, her muddy chin dropping to her chest. All of this terror and pain because of her brother's selfish and criminal acts.

"You're hit?" Rhy asked.

Her head snapped up. "Who's hit?"

"His bullet grazed my arm, it's nothing." Brady pulled out his phone. "I need Neal's last name."

"Josling. Neal Josling." Grace shakily rose to her feet. "Let me see your injury."

"I'm fine," Brady repeated. He turned his attention to making the call. "This is FBI Agent Brady Finnegan, reporting a shooting at 1735 Domingo Road in Brookland. Perp is Neal Josling, and he's been shot."

"Tell them to hurry," Rhy advised. "I hit him in the center of his chest. Not sure how long he has."

Taken out the very same way Neal had shot Parker Hall. Grace couldn't help thinking it was divine justice at work. A life for a life.

Then again, the sixth of God's Ten Commandments was *Thou shall not kill.*

Brady relayed the urgency of the situation, then disconnected from the call. His gaze clung to hers. "Are you all right? You're not hurt?"

She rubbed at the mud clinging to her chin. "I'm fine, thanks to you."

"Thanks to Rhy," Brady corrected. He looked toward his brother. "What made you come out at that moment?"

"I don't know." Rhy shrugged. "I just had this feeling you shouldn't be outside while this guy was still on the loose."

"I never expected him to be hiding in the backyard."

Brady's voice held disgust. "I should have cleared the area first."

"Hey, things happen for a reason." Rhy shrugged. "This must have been part of God's plan. I'm just glad I decided to carry my weapon. If I hadn't, things would have ended very differently."

"This is my fault," Grace whispered. "I should have thought of Neal as a possible suspect. I didn't know his mother had invested in Adam's scam, but I should have remembered that Neal knew about Caleb being Brady's son. I thought Caleb's good Samaritan leaked the information, but it must have been Neal."

"The blame rests solely on Neal not you," Brady said firmly. "I hope he survives long enough to be arrested and charged with murder, kidnapping, and extortion."

"Do you think he was working alone?" Rhy pressed his hands on Neal's chest, using all his weight to apply pressure to Neal's wound. "Maybe we should put a BOLO out on his mother."

"And his mother's husband," Grace added. "She's divorced and remarried. I—uh, think her name is Helen. I don't remember her last name. I'm not sure what her husband's name is either."

"We'll find her. This isn't your fault, Grace," Brady repeated. "Neal came up with the kidnapping idea. He hired his cousin Parker Hall. You don't own your brother's crimes."

Logically, she knew he was right, but seeing the dark blood staining Brady's sleeve made her feel responsible for this mess. She'd tried to do the right thing by turning her brother in to the Securities Exchange Commission.

Now a man was dead, and another was clinging to life.

"Marc? We have Neal Josling here, he admitted to being the mastermind behind the kidnapping scheme. Claims his mother lost her life savings to Adam Ramsey's investment scam. We need to issue a BOLO for her once we have her last name, first name is Helen. I may have seen her name on the list, under a Helen Singer. If they're the same person, they lost just over a million dollars. I didn't put them high on the list since the ransom demand was significantly more than that."

The additional information Brady revealed was sobering. Neal might claim he was motivated by getting what his mother deserved, but it was pure greed that had been his true motivation. Maybe sparked by his mother's loss, but more so because he wanted money and saw her young son as the easiest way to get it.

Police sirens grew louder as the cops responded to the call. She glanced up at the house, hoping Caleb was sleeping through all of this. She saw Elly's face in a window, and the youngest Finnegan waved her hand, assuring her things inside were okay.

Brookland officers came into the backyard, making sure things were under control before waving the ambulance crew in.

"Hey, it's not every day I get to respond to my family home," a male voice said dryly.

"Nice of you to drop in, Colin," Rhy said dryly. "What are you doing in Brookland? You work downtown, don't you?"

"I fill in once in a while here too," Colin said.

"Great. You wanna take over for me here?" Rhy asked. "He's bleeding bad."

Colin and a female paramedic brought a gurney and box of medical supplies over to where Rhy was still leaning on Neal. The back porch light came on, providing additional illumination for the team.

"Agent Finnegan?" An officer approached Brady. "You want to tell us what happened?"

Grace moved over to stand beside him, ready to chime in as needed.

"You heard the Amber Alert earlier today, right?" Brady asked. "Neal Josling is the man responsible. His mother, Helen, lost money in Adam Ramsey's investment scam. He was looking to replace her loss and to extort more money for himself."

"How did he end up with a bullet to the chest?" the officer asked.

"Neal came out from behind the tree with a gun." Grace picked up the story thread. "He admitted to hiring his cousin Parker Hall to take my son and was irritated that Caleb was under protection. His new plan was to kidnap me as a way to get the money to be transferred into his offshore account."

"My brother MPD Captain Rhyland Finnegan came outside in the nick of time," Brady said. "He told us to get down as Neal fired at me, grazing my upper arm. Rhy fired in return, taking him out."

"That's awfully convenient," the officer muttered.

She narrowed her gaze and stepped closer. "My son was kidnapped and held against his will for over thirteen hours. Then we were held at gunpoint by the same man who ruthlessly took him. Brady was shot in the arm trying to rescue me! I don't think that's convenient at all; in fact, this entire day has been a complete nightmare."

"Okay, okay." The officer held up a hand. "I didn't mean to insinuate that this hasn't been a terrible ordeal."

"It has been, and that man"—she jerked her thumb to

where Colin and the female paramedic were working on Neal—"is responsible for every painful second of it. After everything we've been through, he had the audacity to attempt to kidnap me right from the Finnegans' backyard!"

"Easy, Grace." Brady slipped his good arm around her waist. "Asking questions and gathering information is part of the job."

Her flash of anger dissipated, leaving her feeling weak and shaky. Still, she wasn't at all satisfied. "If that's the case, they should be nicer about it. We are not the bad guys here. Neal is. And if you ask me, he got exactly what he deserved."

The officers looked at each other as if unsure what to say.

The corner of Brady's mouth curved up in a smile. "Don't poke the mamma bear."

Rhy joined them, Neal's blood staining his hands. He gestured to the ground. "That's my weapon, you'll need it to compare it with the bullet embedded in Josling's chest."

"Yeah, thanks." The one officer looked happy to have something constructive to do.

"Oh, and Josling's weapon is in the brush near the tree," Rhy added. "I kicked it out of the way."

"I think we have enough information for now," the officer who'd taken the lead said. "I appreciate your cooperation. It's clear Josling was trespassing and that he had a gun. I would ask that you stick around and provide your contact information. We may need to clarify a few details later."

"I live here," Rhy said. "Brady and Grace will be staying for the next few days too. And of course, we'll provide our phone numbers. We're happy to cooperate in any way."

"Thanks." The officer turned away just as Colin and his

partner wheeled Neal past them. The grim expression on their faces indicated Neal's condition was tenuous.

She couldn't bring herself to care. Maybe that made her a horrible person, but it was difficult to forgive him for terrorizing her son.

"Another day at the Finnegan homestead," Rhy drawled. "Never a dull moment around here."

Brady chuckled. "Yeah, no kidding. I feel bad about this, Rhy. But I thank God you came out when you did."

"Glad to help. Let's get your arm taken care of." Rhy grimaced. "We can ask Elly to take a look, although I get the sense she is still a bit squeamish about bloody wounds."

"Squeamish?" Grace frowned. "Isn't she an EMT?"

"Yeah, my point exactly." Rhy shrugged. "If this career doesn't work out, she can try something else."

"This is her fourth career choice," Brady pointed out. "At some point she needs to settle into a role and stick to it."

"I know, but she insists on joining the family legacy of being a first responder. I've tried to convince her that other careers are just as noble." Rhy sighed heavily. "Not everyone is cut out to bolt toward danger rather than running away. And I'm afraid that is the core of Elly's problem."

"I'm not cut out for that type of work either," Grace said. "But I am used to doing first aid on kids who fall and cut themselves all the time. I'll clean up your arm, Brady."

"Thanks." Brady opened the door for them so Rhy wouldn't have to touch it with his bloody hands.

As Rhy washed up at the kitchen sink, Devon came over. "I heard the gunfire but stayed inside the way you asked." Her eyes widened at the blood swirling in the sink.

"It's not mine," Rhy hastened to assure his wife. "Brady suffered a minor wound, but otherwise, we're okay."

"Thank You, God," Devon whispered.

"Amen to that," Brady added. He dropped into a chair at the kitchen table. "Devon, will you grab the first aid kit Alanna put together for us?"

"Yes." Devon disappeared, returning a few minutes later with a large plastic box. It was twice the size of the first aid kit she kept at the Rising Star day care center, but that one hadn't been put together by an ER nurse.

Brady peeled off his shirt, revealing an ugly gash on his arm. Thankfully, it wasn't as deep as she feared. Keeping her gaze averted from his muscular physique wasn't easy. She cleaned the wound, applied antibiotic cream, then wrapped gauze around his upper bicep.

When she finished, she sank into the chair closest to him. "It's finally over," she whispered.

"Yes." Brady put his uninjured arm around her and pulled her close. "I can't believe you were going to sacrifice yourself, Grace."

"I had to." The reality of the near miss hit hard. At the time, she had been determined to keep Neal from shooting Brady. "I took some comfort in knowing Caleb would be safe with you and the rest of the Finnegan family."

Even if that meant leaving Caleb forever.

THE WAY GRACE had stepped toward Neal had shaved ten years from his life. He had not been prepared for that.

"Grace." He turned in his seat so he could draw her closer. "I told you I would never take Caleb away. Not now, not ever."

"I believe you." Her simple admission warmed his heart. "But seeing Neal only reinforced that this mess started with me. With my brother. And obviously with my brief and ill-fated relationship with Neal."

"He's no longer a threat, Grace. You and Caleb are safe now." He wanted to check with Callahan to see if Neal's mother and stepfather had been found yet, but he didn't want to let go of Grace long enough to make the call. "I would have given my life for you because Caleb needs you. He doesn't even know me."

"Not yet, but he will." Grace shook her head, her expression pained. "I should have let you tell him the truth earlier. I guess deep down I wanted one more night to have him all to myself."

"We can wait as long as you like." It wasn't easy to give that up, but telling Caleb he was the boy's father wasn't nearly as important as Grace. "I want you to be ready. To have faith that we will work together to care for him."

"You would do that for me?" She looked up at him in surprise.

"Grace, haven't you figured out yet how much I love you?" He hadn't meant to sound so exasperated. "You are very important to me. And so is Caleb. I take responsibility for not coming to check on you seven years ago when I was finished with my training. Especially after I was assigned to work here in the FBI Milwaukee office, the way I'd requested. I should have headed to Chicago to find you."

"Are you sure?" There was a hint of hope in her green eyes, yet her tone conveyed doubt. "I'm finding it hard to believe you've forgiven me for what I've done."

"I was very angry at first." There was no reason to lie about that. "I did resent you for keeping me from knowing my son."

"See? That's exactly what I mean."

"You didn't let me finish," he chided. "God asks us to

forgive those who trespass against us. And, Grace, I very much believe God brought us together now for a reason. Partially so I could help support you during the kidnapping and assist in getting Caleb back. But even more so, it's possible we weren't ready to be together back then. That we both had to grow up a bit more before coming together."

She searched his gaze for a long moment. "I want to believe you, Brady. But I keep thinking that none of this would have happened if I hadn't kept Caleb a secret."

"You can't think like that. It's not for us to question God's plan."

She frowned. "Okay, but we haven't been together for seven years. We're different people now than we were back then."

"Yes, we are. We're older, wiser, and hopefully better equipped to provide Caleb the love he needs." He was getting the impression she did not love him the way he loved her. "It's okay, Grace. You don't have to make any sort of commitment to me, I understand this is all very sudden. Just agree to one thing, that we'll work together to create a loving atmosphere for our son."

"I promise," Grace whispered. "Caleb needs a father figure in his life. And I know he'll benefit from being part of the Finnegan family."

He wanted so badly to assure her she was part of their family, just by being Caleb's mother. But he didn't want to push any more than he had. It wasn't Grace's fault she didn't love him. You couldn't force that on someone.

"Thank you." Brady pressed a chaste kiss to her temple. "We should try to get some sleep."

Grace rested against him without moving. He held her close, in no rush to leave. If this was as much as she was comfortable with, he'd take it.

Gladly.

His phone rang, interrupting the moment. Seeing Marc's name on the screen, he quickly answered. "Hey, Marc. Did you find them?"

"Sure did." Satisfaction rang in Marc's voice. "You were right, Helen and Steve Singer were on the victim list. Our Chicago team found them at home watching television. It doesn't appear as if they were involved in the kidnapping plot, but the Chicago feds took them in for questioning."

"That's the second best news all night," Brady said. "I hope Neal Josling pulls through long enough to spend the rest of his life in prison."

"Yeah, I'm with you on that." Marc was silent for a moment. "I'm glad it's over, Brady. I hope Grace and Caleb can get through this."

"I hope so too." Grace lifted her head to look up at him. Maybe she'd heard Marc's comment. He smiled and said, "Thanks again, Marc. I appreciate the way you've had my back today."

"I called Donovan to let him know," Marc said. "I told him you were injured and would touch base with him tomorrow. He's already mentioned wanting our reports first thing."

The bureau was ever fond of its paperwork. "I will get those reports done, thanks." Calling his boss had never crossed his mind. His main concern was Grace and Caleb.

"Chat with you tomorrow." Marc disconnected from the call.

"It's really over." Grace sounded relieved. "Neal's mother wasn't part of it after all, even though she was the one to lose all that money." She sighed and ran her fingers through her hair. "I'm glad Neal dreamed this up on his own."

He was glad to know Neal would never hurt anyone ever again. "You're exhausted. Let's head upstairs. I'll walk you to your room."

She rose, then turned to face him rather than going for the stairs. "I love you too, Brady."

"You do?" He sounded like an idiot. "I don't want you to say that just because I did. Your feelings one way or the other won't change how we co-parent Caleb." He didn't want her to feel as if she had to stay with him because of their son.

"That's not it," she said. "I couldn't make myself care about Neal; our relationship ended within weeks because I couldn't get you out of my mind. He said it was fine to remain friends, which was a huge relief." She shook her head. "I know I've made a complete mess of this, but one thing has never changed. My feelings for you."

He desperately wanted to believe her. "We'll take things slow and easy. No reason to rush. We have plenty of time, Grace. I want you to be sure about this." He flushed and added, "I rushed you once seven years ago, the night we created Caleb. I won't make that mistake again."

Her low, husky laugh caught him off guard. "It's sweet that you think you rushed me that night." She wound her arms around his neck. "The truth is I wanted you, Brady. I was an equal partner that night. And I don't regret a minute of it because Caleb is an amazing little boy."

He wasn't sure what to say, he knew he should have been more responsible, but she was right. Their son was amazing.

He kissed her. This time there was no evil kidnapper to interrupt. But Elly soon found them. The constant family members coming and going was one of the reasons he'd left the homestead as soon as he could.

This was a perfect example.

"Oh, hey." Elly smiled cheekily. "Sorry to barge in without knocking."

Brady sighed. "There's no door on the kitchen, El."

"Yeah, well, what can I say? I have rotten timing." His sister laughed. "I thought I'd let you know Caleb is still asleep. He hasn't suffered any nightmares yet."

"Thank you, Elly." Grace turned in his arms. "You were wonderful to stay close to him."

"Hey, what's with Alanna's first aid kit?" Elly's gaze darted to the gauze Grace had wrapped around his upper arm. Elly paled, and for a moment, Brady feared she'd faint. "You were hurt? Why didn't you tell me?"

"I'm fine, it's just a scratch," he assured her. "There was no need to bother the new family EMT for something so minor."

"I—uh, am glad to hear it." Elly visibly swallowed hard.

"The danger is over," Brady continued, thinking it was the aspect of danger that had hit her so hard. "The bad guys are gone and never coming back. No need to be concerned, okay?"

"Great news." Elly's smile didn't reach her eyes. "I'm heading upstairs. Good night, you two."

"Good night," Brady and Grace answered at the same time.

When they were alone again, Brady sneaked another quick kiss. After being away from her for so long, he couldn't seem to get enough of her. "I love you so much, Grace. I thank God for bringing you back into my life."

"I love you too," Grace whispered. She smiled and kissed him again before stepping back. The sound of a boy crying out in fear had her whirling toward the stairs. "Come with me, Brady. Caleb will need both of us to reassure him that he's safe."

A sweet offer that he quickly grabbed with both hands. "Absolutely. Let's go."

Together they rushed up the stairs to comfort their son. As Grace tucked Caleb between them on the bed, Brady lifted his eyes to the ceiling and silently thanked God for this special gift.

His family.

EPILOGUE

Four weeks later . . .

Grace closed the Rising Star day care center for the day as Caleb played with the Thor action figure Brady had gotten for him the day he'd been rescued. It had soon become his favorite, to the point he'd gotten into a fight with his best friend Charlie when the other boy had tried to take it.

"Mine," Caleb had said, snatching it back. "My daddy gave it to me."

"You're supposed to share," Charlie had protested. "You can play with my Aquaman."

"Don't wanna." Caleb thrust his lower lip out in a pout. "I like Thor better than Aquaman."

"Your father would want you to share, Caleb," she'd told him. "Remember?"

Caleb had acted as if he hadn't heard her, clutching Thor to his chest protectively. Charlie had given up and walked away.

The three of them—Caleb, Brady, and Grace—had attended family counseling twice a week since the incident.

Over the past four weeks, Caleb's nightmares had dwindled from being a nightly occurrence to every other week.

Soon, she hoped, they'd go away forever.

"Daddy!" Most days, unless he was involved in a big case, Brady came to pick them up at the end of the day. Fridays were extra special because they had dinner together.

"Hey, champ." Brady swung Caleb into his arms for a hug and a kiss. "I hope you were a good boy today."

Caleb looked back at her, then hung his head. "Charlie wanted to play with Thor, but I wouldn't let him."

Brady sighed. "Caleb, we had this discussion. You need to share your toys with your friend Charlie. And the other kids too."

"I know," Caleb mumbled. Then the little boy perked up. "But I didn't tell Mommy our secret."

Secret? She raised a brow as Brady winced. "You're not supposed to mention the secret, remember?"

Caleb comically clapped his hands over his mouth.

"Ready to go?" Brady asked. He held Caleb as Grace grabbed her purse and pulled out her keys.

Outside, she locked the door, then walked with Brady and Caleb to his SUV. "What secret?"

"You'll see." Brady frowned at Caleb. "We're not going to tell until we get to the restaurant, right?"

"Right." Caleb grinned. "You're going to love it, Mom."

"Come on, kid, you're killing me," Brady muttered as he put the boy in the booster seat.

She hid a smile at his frustration. The past four weeks had been wonderful, with Grace and Caleb spending two nights during the week at Brady's condo, along with the weekends. Her apartment had been repaired, with a new security system installed, but she couldn't deny that living in the small one-room place wasn't nearly as nice as spending time with Brady.

Their favorite restaurant, one that served pizza as well as nicer Italian food, wasn't far. They were becoming Friday night regulars; the staff always brightened and welcomed them by name when they arrived.

"This way, please, Mr. Finnegan," the hostess said as she carried their menus to a small booth in the back. "Tina, your server, will be with you shortly."

"Thank you," Brady said.

Grace had Caleb crawl in first, before sliding into the booth. She'd no sooner taken her seat when Brady abruptly dropped to one knee and pulled out a small ring box.

"Grace, since Caleb pretty much spilled the beans, I figure I should ask now rather than wait for dessert. Will you please marry me?"

She ignored the looks they were getting from the other patrons of the restaurants. She couldn't imagine a more perfect proposal. "Yes, Brady. I'd love to marry you."

"I told you she'd like it." Caleb bounced in the seat. "I knew she'd like the sparkly ring."

Brady laughed ruefully. "I asked Caleb for permission to marry you. You should know he heartily approved."

"Oh, Brady." She stood, drew him up, and kissed him. "I can't wait until we're all Finnegans."

"I can't wait until we add to the Finnegan family," Brady whispered. He kissed her, then slipped the ring on her finger. "I love you, Grace."

"And I love you too." She turned to look at their son. "We can add to the family if I get a little girl next time."

Brady laughed. "No promises. You realize there are six boys and only three girls in the entire Finnegan family."

"Well, then, we'll just have to practice until we get it right."

"I'm on board with that idea," he murmured.

She grinned, then slid back into the booth. "Shall we order? I'm hungry."

"I want pizza!" Caleb announced.

"That's nothing new," Brady said dryly. "You might want to switch things up once in a while."

"I like pizza," Caleb argued. "It's my favorite!"

Grace looked from the man she'd promised to marry to the little boy they'd created together.

Brady had been right all along. God had brought them together for a reason. And while she knew there would be ups and downs, Brady was the right man to walk at her side through each sunny and stormy day.

Together, forever.

I HOPE you enjoyed reading Brady and Grace's story in *Midnight Abduction*. The Finnegan family has been so much fun to write. Are you ready to read Quinn and Sami's story in *Risky Rescue*? Click here!

DEAR READER

I hope you're enjoying my Finnegan First Responders series. I'm having so much fun writing the story for each Finnegan sibling, along with revisiting the Callahans. I cannot wait to have the big family gathering at the end of the series.

If you enjoyed reading about Brady and Grace in *Midnight Abduction*, take a moment to check out Quinn and Sami's story in *Risky Rescue*. Don't forget you can purchase e-books and audiobooks directly from my website and will receive a 15% discount by using the code **LauraScott15**. My e-books are available on my website before they are released on all other platforms.

I adore hearing from my readers! I can be found through my website at https://www.laurascottbooks.com, via Facebook at https://www.facebook.com/LauraScott Books, Instagram at https://www.instagram.com/laurascott books/, and Twitter https://twitter.com/laurascottbooks. Also, take a moment to sign up for my monthly newsletter to learn about my new book releases! All subscribers receive a free novella not available for purchase on any platform.

Until next time,
Laura Scott

RISKY RESCUE

Chapter One

Sami Lopez, a.k.a. Angelina Morales, threw a worried glance over her shoulder. She couldn't see anyone following her, but the dark clouds rolling in made it difficult to be sure. She was still reeling over the events that had taken place on shore. Her cover had been blown, in the worst way possible.

The strong scent of gasoline wafted toward her. Not an unusual scent while out on a low-slung speedboat, but it was strong enough to give her pause. She'd spent her teenage years on the water and in boats, but there was no denying that while she was speeding across Lake Michigan, a lake that was over twenty-two-hundred square miles across, the inability to see either shoreline was unnerving.

She was literally in the middle of the lake where the depths could reach over nine hundred feet. The wind kicked up, the dark clouds swirling fast along the horizon bringing another rush of concern. The gasoline scent grew stronger.

Something was wrong.

As a Drug Enforcement Agent working undercover, Sami had long since learned to trust her gut. Bad enough things had spiraled out of control when she'd left Cambridge, Michigan, and now this? The situation had gone from bad to worse.

She wanted to take a closer look at the large Mercury Marine engine on her boat's stern, but the impending storm would not make that an easy task. Cutting back on the speed, she fought hard to keep the bow of the craft pointing west. Her ultimate destination was the small town of Shady Lane, located about fifty miles outside of Milwaukee along the Wisconsin shoreline.

At least, that had been the plan. Now she'd take just about any city along the coast of Wisconsin as long as she made it there alive.

"Come on, come on," she told herself, the wind making it impossible to hear her own voice. "You can do this!"

The boat engine abruptly sputtered and died. Without the engine to power the craft, the wind took control, buffeting the low-slung boat from side to side, threatening to dump her up and over the edge.

She wore a life jacket, but there were no other boats around as far as she could see. The average temperature of Lake Michigan in the summer, even early July, was 72 degrees. How long would she be able to survive in the water before hypothermia claimed her?

No, don't think about it. Grabbing the radio, she flipped the switch to call for help.

There was nothing but dead air. Not even static.

Alarm skittered across her skin. A huge wave almost knocked her off the boat, but she clung to the wheel and bent over, trying to troubleshoot the radio. Droplets of water stung her eyes, making it difficult to see. The bucking up and down of the boat didn't exactly help either.

Using her fingers, she checked the connection, reaching all the way up into the console. The sharp ends of two wires stabbed her fingertips. It took a moment for her to realize the wires had been cut.

Her radio had been sabotaged!

The scent of gasoline was even stronger now, deepening her sense of apprehension. If the radio had been tampered with, she had little doubt that the engine had been too. She needed to get away! Without hesitation, she kicked off her shoes, stepped up onto the captain's chair, and jumped off the rocking boat, propelling herself as far from the craft as possible, into the white-capped waves.

Breaking the surface, she gasped for air. The waves were much higher than she'd anticipated, crashing over her head and dunking her deeper into the depths of the second largest of the Great Lakes.

Swimming was her strong suit, she'd won several medals in high school and college, but that was in long Olympic-length pools, not choppy lake water in the middle of a storm. Still, she had confidence in her ability. Sputtering, she quickly pulled the chained buoy toward her. Tucking it under her chest, she used it to keep her higher above the water level as she did her best to swim away from the boat, silently praying for Jesus to keep her safe from harm.

She hadn't gotten very far when a loud explosion rocked the air. Sami instinctively turned onto her back, lifting her arm to protect her head, when a chunk of fiberglass sailed toward her.

Then there was nothing but darkness.

"LIEUTENANT FINNEGAN? We—report of an explosion—roughly twenty nautical miles from your location." The voice over the radio was occasionally broken up by static. The storm on the horizon was wreaking havoc with the transmission. "Requesting—on scene to determine —rescue efforts."

"Ten-four," Quinn Finnegan said curtly. "Unit twelve responding." He pushed the throttle of the Coast Guard cutter forward, sending the boat leaping over the choppy waves. An explosion was hardly a normal call, although much of the summer months were spent in rescue efforts.

Boat engines didn't just blow up. Every one of Quinn's senses was on red alert. Was this some sort of trap? The Coast Guard was a highly competitive branch of the military, one he proudly served. But over the past few years, more and more boats were being used to transport drugs. And no one hated the Coast Guard more than drug runners.

He reached for the radio again. "Dispatch? Who called in the report of the explosion?"

"The captain—charter fishing boat" came the response. "They saw it in the distance as they were heading back to shore."

"Ten-four." Quinn decided he'd have to size up the situation once they got there. His partner, Callum Jenkins, came up to stand beside him.

"What was that about an explosion?" Cal shouted above the wind.

"Report was called in by a charter fishing boat." He didn't glance at his junior ensign, his gaze glued to the horizon. In the distance, he could see a ball of orange bobbing in the water.

Was that their target? Probably. The wind buffeted

their Coast Guard cutter, but he didn't slacken his speed, using all his strength to hold the wheel steady, keeping them on course. If there were survivors in the boat or in the water, they were likely injured.

Or dead.

Having been raised as a Christian, and still attending church with his eight siblings when he wasn't scheduled to work or deployed to wherever the Coast Guard sent him, he was very familiar with the concept of forgiveness and redemption. That didn't mean he had much sympathy for drug runners. He despised the poison they spread, especially the younger crowd. Deaths from Fentanyl were on the rise, especially among teenagers. The synthetic drug was easy to make and cheap to buy. It made him sick to know the occupants of the boat might be involved in that. Yet who those people were or what they did wasn't the point. His job was to rescue anyone in need.

Besides, he could be wrong. The boat could belong to a couple of kids who thought it would be fun to take a joy ride despite the impending storm.

Yet that wouldn't explain the explosion. In his experience, boat engines didn't just explode. Not without help.

The ball of orange grew bigger and brighter as they raced toward it. Quinn scanned the surface of the lake, searching for survivors. He didn't see anything, but in water this choppy, he would need to get closer to know for sure. Even if the victims were wearing life jackets, finding them bobbing beneath the waves wouldn't be easy.

Based on the velocity of the wind, calling for the Coast Guard chopper wasn't an option. He and Cal would just have to haul any possible survivors in by themselves.

Adrenaline surged as the cutter drew closer to the

wreckage. He could see that the entire stern of the boat was engulfed in flames.

No one was behind the wheel. It was possible the captain had been knocked unconscious during the explosion and was lying along the bottom of the vessel.

"I don't see anyone, do you?" Cal asked.

"Negative." The moment the word left his mouth, he spotted something bobbing in the water on the opposite side of the craft. It wasn't the usual reflector on a life jacket, but it was definitely a person. "There, do you see it? One victim overboard. Keep your eyes peeled for others."

"Yes, sir."

Quinn pulled back on the throttle, bringing their speed down. Cranking on the wheel, he made a wide berth around the damaged boat to approach the victim. He didn't dare go any faster, lest there be other victims floating nearby. But he didn't see anyone else.

When he was roughly forty yards away from the bobbing person in the water, he throttled back, putting the cutter in reverse for a moment to slow their momentum. The victim didn't wave or acknowledge their presence, giving him a sense of dread.

Was he already dead?

"Cal, man the wheel." He waited until the young ensign stepped forward to take his place, then shifted out of the way. "I'm going in after him."

"Sir?" Cal sounded alarmed. "Are you sure about this?"

"Yes." Someone had to jump into the lake, and Quinn had five years of experience over the younger man. Even though he was only thirty years old, there were times he felt downright ancient. "Your job is to hold her steady, understand? And look for other survivors."

"Yes, sir!"

The kid looked overwhelmed, but Quinn trusted Cal to follow orders. The Coast Guard was a competitive branch of the military. They only took the best of the best. The fact that this kid was with him now meant he'd already passed rigorous training.

Granted, they'd been riding together for the past two months without ever experiencing a rescue like this.

Double-checking his gear, Quinn moved to the aft side of the vessel. Up ahead he could see the victim still bobbing in the water, head tilted to the side as if the person was unconscious. On one hand, he was glad to be hauling in someone who didn't fight you with every stroke.

He just hoped the victim was still alive.

As he prepared to jump overboard, the skies above opened, sending a deluge of rain down upon them. The wind kicked up, the rain stinging his eyes, making it difficult to see. The rain would help keep the boat fire under control, but it would have the opposite effect on his rescue efforts.

The wind and the rain would make it much more difficult to get to the victim before he drowned.

Quinn jumped off the edge of the cutter, steeling himself as the cold water enveloped him. He was already drenched from the rain, but the lake water was cold against his skin. He took a moment to gather the rope with the red Coast Guard life preserver ring attached to it. Then he struck out in a side stroke in the direction of the victim.

Between the water pummeling him from above and the waves crashing into his face, he was breathless by the time he managed to get within fifteen feet of the victim. Tossing his head to get water off his face, he eyed the victim.

Dark hair was plastered around a face with dainty features. A dark gash over the left side of her forehead indicated she was injured.

Or worse.

He kicked his legs, propelling himself closer. His training was such that he knew it wasn't a good idea to get too close to a victim. Drowning people had been known to drag their rescuers down in a surge of panic.

But the way the rain pounded her face, without any movement from her, made him think that wouldn't be a problem. "Hey!" he shouted against the wind. "I'm Lieutenant Finnegan with the Coast Guard! Can you hear me?"

She didn't move. Didn't lift her head or acknowledge him in any way.

He continued swimming closer, noticing the wide section of fiberglass floating a few yards away from his victim. After several powerful kicks, he finally managed to reach the woman's side.

She'd been smart enough to have a buoy clipped to her life vest. The small beacon on the vest, though, was broken, maybe a result of the explosion. Or the fiberglass wreckage. He had no idea what had transpired before he'd arrived.

He quickly searched for a pulse, silently praying she wasn't dead. With the rain getting in his eyes, he couldn't see her clearly to verify that she was breathing.

Her skin was cold and clammy beneath his touch. A large wave rolled over them, making him sputter. His fingers found her carotid artery, and he was reassured to feel the faint beat of her heart.

At least he wouldn't have to do CPR while hauling her back to the cutter. Relieved, he turned the victim so that her back was facing him. Blinking against the rain, he fought a momentary surge of panic when he didn't immediately see the cutter.

There! He swallowed hard, realizing it was almost fifty

yards away. Maybe Cal didn't trust himself to get any closer.

Quinn took a deep breath and began swimming again, slowly bringing his female victim along. It didn't seem possible, but the waves were getting worse now, crashing over him and the woman he was towing toward the Coast Guard boat with such velocity he feared they wouldn't make it. The high waves forced him to glance back at her, to make sure the woman's face was clear and not submerged in water.

The fact that she didn't cough made him worry she wasn't breathing. And if that was the case, her pulse wouldn't last long. He kicked his legs again and again, but the cutter didn't seem to be getting any closer.

Out of nowhere, a second explosion rocked the night. He instinctively ducked his head while reaching behind to pull the woman's head and upper torso closer to his body to protect her from falling debris.

Bits and pieces of fiberglass and boat parts pelted the lake water around them. Something hard struck his arm, sending pain zinging through him.

They weren't going to make it!

As soon as the thought entered his mind, Quinn shoved it out. They would make it. Failure was not an option.

Please, Lord Jesus, keep us safe!

The silent prayer brought a sense of calm, soothing his nerves. When he was convinced that they were clear of any more flying debris, he shifted the woman back into a rescue hold. Then he struck out swimming again, pushing himself harder than ever, kicking with as much strength as he could muster.

He had to get this woman to the cutter!

Quinn had no idea how long he and his victim had been

in the lake, or how much water he'd swallowed, but soon the lights of the cutter came into view. He hoped the beacon on his vest was bright enough for Cal to see through the rain. He needed his young partner to help him get the woman up and into the vessel.

"Lieutenant!" Cal shouted. "Do you want me to send down the skid?"

The skid was a long flotation device they used to bring unconscious victims into the boat. Fighting the waves and the wind had sapped his strength, but Quinn didn't think he needed to use the skid. The woman didn't weigh that much from what he could tell.

"I've got her." Three more powerful kicks brought him to the edge of the boat. He reached up and grasped the ladder, holding it for a moment to catch his breath. The waves continued to batter him, slamming him up against the side of the cutter. He tightened his grip in sheer determination.

He could do this!

Getting his feet under him, he propped them on the lower rung of the ladder. Then he used one arm to pull himself upward, holding on to the victim with the other. He drew the woman up with him, one rung of the ladder at a time until he was close enough to the top where Cal waited.

"I need you—to grab her," he said between panting breaths.

"Yes, sir!" Cal bent over the side, grabbed the woman's life jacket, and hauled her the rest of the way up and into the boat.

Thank you, Lord! Relief washed over him as he managed to climb the last few ladder rungs to get to safety. He almost fell on his face, his legs giving out from exertion.

The rain continued to pelt him in the face, though, so lying on the deck wasn't an option. He rolled to his knees, took another deep breath, and pushed himself to his feet. Thankfully, his muscles seemed to cooperate by supporting him. He shivered as he hobbled over to where Cal had carried the woman into the cabin of the vessel to protect her from the rain.

Grabbing a towel from the stack stored on every cutter, he swiped it over his head and face, then draped it over his shoulders. Ignoring the gash on his arm, he knelt on the other side of the woman as Cal removed her life jacket and buoy.

Alarm raised the hair on the back of his neck. "Does she still have a pulse?"

"Yes, but she's not breathing."

"I'll give her rescue breaths; you grab the medical supplies. There's an Ambu Bag and mask in there." Without waiting for Cal's response, Quinn bent and gave the woman two rescue breaths.

Nothing.

He tried again, giving two more breaths. She abruptly threw up, gagging as her lungs expelled the water she'd inhaled. He quickly turned her onto her side, using the edge of the towel to wipe her face.

Now that he could see the victim more clearly, he realized she looked familiar.

"I've got it," Cal said breathlessly, setting the large red box beside him.

"Thanks, but we don't need it. She's okay." Coughing like crazy but otherwise okay. "Take the wheel, Cal. Take the boat around the boat to see if you see other survivors just in case their reflector signals were damaged too. If not, get us back to shore, pronto."

"You sure?" Cal's eyes brightened at the opportunity to drive the boat.

"Go, hurry." Quinn searched for another towel and used it to pat the woman's damp hair. Then he grabbed a foil blanket to combat hypothermia. "You okay, ma'am? What's your name?"

She was still coughing, her face turned away from him. It took her several minutes to regain her composure. Pushing herself into a sitting position, she took the towel from him and buried her face in the cotton fabric. He draped the foil blanket around her, making her look like a skinny baked potato.

Then she raised her head to look at him. In that moment, he realized she was his former fiancée, Sami Lopez.

His mouth dropped open in shock. This couldn't be right. Sami was dead! Two years ago, he and Sami had been planning their wedding. Then she'd abruptly told him she couldn't marry him. She'd returned his ring and told him she had to go to California. Just weeks later, he'd heard she'd died in the line of duty while in LA. Her obituary was still in his home office.

Yet here he was looking right at her.

"Sami? What in the world happened? I thought you were dead! Were you on the boat by yourself? Or are there other victims we should be searching for?" He knew he was peppering her with questions, but he needed answers.

"I—don't know." A look of confusion crossed her features. She looked away from him, her gaze taking in her surroundings. "You're with the Coast Guard?"

"Yes." He frowned. Sami knew full well he was with the Coast Guard. They'd struggled at times to make their schedules work, but he'd thought they were okay.

But they weren't. Sami had made that perfectly clear.

It was even more shocking, though, to realize she wasn't dead.

The cutter buffeted with the wind. In the distance he saw another cutter heading toward the burning boat. "I need to know who else I need to be out there searching for!" He didn't bother to hide his exasperation. "You know as well as I do that it's dangerous to take a boat out all by yourself, especially this far from shore."

"I—uh, don't think there's anyone else." She did not sound the least bit convincing. The dazed confusion was still in her dark eyes, and she lifted a hand to gingerly touch the wound on her forehead. "My head hurts."

"I'm sure it does." He stared at her for a long moment. Sami didn't usually avoid direct questions. She'd been a cop and had never hesitated to put herself in danger. The way she was looking around, as if she had no idea who he was, rankled.

Two years wasn't that long. He didn't think he'd changed that much.

Was it possible this woman wasn't Sami? He'd heard everyone had a twin somewhere in the world.

Yet he knew this was Sami. "Come on, Sami. Talk to me. Tell me what happened." He gentled his tone, hoping to reassure her. "You're safe now."

"Am I?" She frowned. "I would like to tell you what happened, but I don't know."

He stared at her. "You must know. You were there. On the boat. What happened? Do you have any idea why the engine exploded?"

"Boat engines don't just explode," she said.

Swallowing another surge of frustration, he said, "Yeah,

I know. Which is why I need to understand what happened?"

Wincing, she dropped her hand to her lap. "Honestly, I'd like to help you. But I don't remember."

A chill that had nothing to do with the weather snaked over him. "You don't remember being on the boat?"

"No." She stared at him for a moment. "I get the sense you know me, you called me Sami. Is that my name?"

The chill coalesced into ice. He held her gaze. "Yes, your full name is Samarita Lopez, you go by Sami. And I'm Quinn Finnegan. You don't remember me either?"

"I'm afraid not." She looked upset. "I'm sorry if we were friends. I don't understand what's happening. Other than my head hurts. I—maybe I'll remember more after I get some rest."

The woman he'd dated for over a year, had been engaged to for another three months, didn't remember her own name. Or him?

And she wasn't dead, the way it had been reported?

Quinn had a bad feeling about this. What had Sami been doing out in the middle of Lake Michigan in a boat that had exploded resulting in her nearly drowning to death?

Made in the USA
Columbia, SC
21 March 2024

33392470R00134